# Stun

# Into A Prayer

WITHDRAWN

An Urban Christian Romance

ayne Colley

# STUMBLING INTO A PRAYER

*IF*
*Colley*

Copyright © 2017 Wayne Colley

## DEDICATION

God is of course the very first person I'd like to give thanks to for giving me the inspiration and drive to write this work. The next group of people I'd like to hank for their support is my family, friends, and fans. t took all of you in order for this book to happen and for it to be successful.

May the good Lord bless each and every one of you all.

## THE STORYLINE

Lisa is a beautiful sista with a good heart. Unfortunately she hasn't had the greatest start to life. She hooks up with a much older boyfriend, who due to his criminal ways, can provide her with all the material possessions that she's ever dreamed of. In time, Lisa comes to realize that the life she's living can leave her in a world of trouble — particularly with the Atlanta Police Department. Fortunately, she begins to dream of a bigger and better future for herself. Maybe by grace, she'll end up with everything she really wants in life — true love included — when she stumbles into God via a prayer.

# STUMBLING INTO A PRAYER

# CHAPTER 1

"I get paid tomorrow and I can't wait to finally go back-to-school shopping, Carmen. Your girl 'bout to be looking cute when I step through the front doors of McKinley High."

Carmen high-fived Lisa. "Ain't nothing wrong with going back to school looking fly, boo. Nothing wrong with that at all."

"I know that's the truth, girl." Lisa laughed.

The next day, Lisa was excited when her money from working at a local bakery showed up in her checking account at the credit union. She couldn't afford a cellphone of her own, so she picked her mama's up from off of the coffee table and used it to go online and check her account. Her mama — Diane — stepped into the living room with Lisa's little brother, Sean, who was only two years old, on her hip.

"You seen my cellphone, Lisa?" Diane asked.

"Yeah." Lisa held the phone up so her mother could see it. "I got it right here. I was using it to see whether or not my paycheck had hit the bank yet."

6

Lisa's mama frowned. "About that, I been meaning to ask you if you could do me a favor."

*Oh, shit,* Lisa thought to herself while wearing an '*I don't believe this*' look on her face. *She bout to ask my ass for some money. I know she is. I just know she is!*

Lisa's mother continued speaking. "The power company is about to turn our electricity off if I don't come up with the past due balance in two days. I hate to ask you... Cause I know you was trying to buy yourself some back-to-school clothes and all—"

Lisa shook her head. "How much is it this time, Mama?"

"Two hundred and eighty-three dollars."

*Damn... That's almost my whole paycheck. I'm only gonna have thirty-eight dollars left.*

Lisa didn't really want to come off of the money, but she loved her mother and her five little brothers and sisters. She didn't want to see them suffering any more than they had to. Lisa's baby brother had asthma. If the electricity was turned off, that would mean that the air conditioner wouldn't work. It was summer and the stifling summer heat always made Shawn's condition worse.

She sighed. "All right, mama." She handed her mother the cellphone. "Log into your electricity company account. I'll pay the bill."

"Thank you, Lisa. I'll pay you back—"

Lisa held out her hand, palm side facing forward,

stopping her mother from speaking. "Um, please don't go there, mama. You still haven't paid me back from when I paid it three months ago. Don't even go there... Okay?"

Diana decided to overlook the offense she felt from the way her oldest child was talking to her. She really felt like saying something like: *Watch your damn mouth, Lisa. I'm the grown-up round here*. But having her seventeen-year-old daughter paying her bills nullified that feeling. It nullified it a whole lot. She wasn't about to bite the hand that was feeding her....well in this case, the hand that was keeping the lights on. She knew it was in her best interest to put some respect on that.

*A Week Later*:

Lisa walked into McKinley High School on the first day of her senior year wearing an outfit from last year. In fact, she wore the very same outfit she'd worn the first day of her junior year. She'd almost made it to first period when she heard a pair of familiar female voices behind her — Tiffany Scott and Angela Anderson.

"Boo, you see what this trick got on?" That was Tiffany speaking. "It's the very same thing she wore on the first day of school last year. Them ten year old Rock & Republic jeans and them Bobo ass looking sneakers."

Tiffany snickered. "Instead of being Jordans, those atrocities on her feet are Lordans… or some other crazy Chinese made up shit."

Lisa had had her entire outfit planned — everything was supposed to have been brand new and literally on and popping. But of course, since she'd used most of her money on paying her mama's electric bill, that hadn't happened. Her outfit was cute, but it paled in comparison to the brand new designer duds and kicks that Tiffany and Angela we're rocking.

This was Lisa's last year of high school, and she'd been putting up with Angela Anderson and Tiffany Scott ever since the three of them had started sixth grade together. She'd had enough of it. Lisa didn't say a word. She balled up her fist, turned around, and popped Tiffany in the mouth.

Tiffany was an uppity and bougie type of girl — in other words, she wasn't used to fighting, even though she was petty and talked a lot of mess. She dropped to the floor from the blow and her girl Angela was too scared to try to do anything. Angela already knew that Lisa and her bestie, Carmen, could and would wipe both her and Tiffany's little bougie heinies. Angela wasn't trying to have anybody's back that day. She wasn't crazy.

Lisa narrowed her eyes at Tiffany. "Next time I bet you gonna watch yo mouth, *trick*." She got pleasure in insulting Tiffany with the very same name she'd just called her.

Yeah, it sure did feel good taking Tiffany Scott out like that. But it came with a price — Lisa got expelled on her very first day of her senior year.

Lisa didn't feel like dealing with school anymore that day, so at a little after nine that morning — right after leaving the principal's office — she left the building and began walking home.

"Hey girl, can I talk to you for a minute?"

Lisa stopped in her tracks as she was walking from the school. She'd heard the car roll up on her and stop, but she wasn't scared or anything because she'd seen it coming out of the corner of her eye and she knew who both the car and the voice belonged to. It belonged to no one other than Ronald Tolliver, a.k.a. Big Ron — one of the baddest drug dealers in her Atlanta neighborhood.

Big Ron was twenty-eight or twenty-nine. Lisa wasn't surprised that he was trying to holler at her because she knew that he liked his women on the young side, he liked keeping it fresh. Word on the street was that his last girlfriend was only sixteen when he'd started dating her. Most normal people would've considered that to be statutory rape — Lisa knew that, she wasn't stupid. But in the hood that Big Ron and Lisa had grown up in, messiness this like that was an everyday thing. It was a common occurrence and nobody really blinked an eye at it.

"Did you hear me, girl?"

Lisa had heard him all right. But acting like she

hadn't was part of the game that she was playing. *Niggas want you even more when you pretty and they they think you trying to diss 'em. It's something about the chase for boss niggas like Big Ron. I seen it go down time and time again with other females out here in these streets.*

She looked through Big Ron's car window at him and gave him a tiny smile. "Um, you talking to me?"

He nodded his head. "Yeah, Shawty. You the only dime out here walking down this sidewalk right now."

"All right. I hear you."

"Won't you at the party down on Madison last weekend?"

She looked him dead in the eye. "I might've been there… Who wants to know?"

Big Ron was kinda arrogant. He considered himself to be the man around town. In his eyes, everybody who was anybody knew him. He frowned and poked out his muscular chest. "I'm Big Ron. I know you heard that name before. Don't act like you ain't, girl."

Yeah Lisa was only seventeen, but she knew how to play the game. She knew if she pushed it any further, all she was gonna do was end up pissing Big Ron off. And she wasn't trying to do that. She liked the finer things in life — even though right now she was living in poverty — and she was sure that with his dope boy money, Big Ron could give her the Gucci, Prada, and Coach that she wanted.

She smiled and nodded her head. "I heard of you all

right. You trying to holler at me or something?"

He grinned. He pressed the button to unlock the door of his custom Benz. "Yeah, girl. Get in."

Lisa became Big Ron's number one chick on that day, not some side ho or number two. Yeah, she knew that he had other women that he was running around with, but that didn't matter to her. All she cared about was the fact that she was his alpha. She came first and she got all the perks that came with being in that position. Money, cars, nice clothes — she had it all. She was sure that the days of having girls like Tiffany Scott pick on her over her clothes were over with.

*Two Years Later*:

Lisa had used to live in the projects with her mama, now she was living with Big Ron in his nice penthouse on the other side of town. Big Ron had just finished hitting it. Since Lisa knew that her man liked smoking a blunt right after they had sex, she threw the bed covers off of her naked body and walked across the room and rolled him a fat one.

Big Ron smiled as he peeped Lisa's naked jiggle as she made her way over to the side table to get his smoke straight.

"You like taking care of yo' man… Don't you, girl?"

"Yep...you know it, daddy."

She fired up the joint and handed it to him. He took a drag and blew out some smoke. "I been thinking 'bout getting out the dope game."

Big Ron spinning the dope game was Lisa's bread-and-butter. So she of course didn't feel like hearing him say that. Her caution radar went from zero to ten in less than a second. "What you mean by *you about to get out the dope game?*"

He chuckled because he knew where she was coming from. "Oh, I'm still gonna be making the big dollars...cause that's what a boss like myself do. I'm just tired of thugging it out there on them streets. I been talking to Don Caprozzi. He getting too old for the gambling business. He owns himself an upscale gambling joint on the outskirts of town. He said he'd sell it to me for a cool three million." Big Ron took another drag from his blunt and nodded his head. "I'm taking him up on his offer. That casino brings in at least twenty million in profit per year."

That sounded okay to Lisa. Big Ron taking care of her was all that really mattered in the end to her. She was sure that the gambling house was probably gonna be an illegal establishment, but she'd turned a blind eye on a whole lot of other sketchy acts that she knew Big Ron had carried out.

*Five Years Later*:

Lisa had long ago gotten tired of sitting around and doing nothing in the mini-mansion that Big Ron had bought for her to live in, so she'd actually asked him if he could get her a job in his casino. Big Ron liked his women on the younger side, so he'd dropped Lisa as his alpha chick. Now pushing twenty-five years old, she knew she was number two — or maybe even three — in his hierarchy of women. But that was all right with Lisa. She preferred it that way because she wasn't in love with Big Ron or anything. In fact, she was starting to look forward to the day where she didn't really have to put up with him. She figured that getting a job in his casino — which paid her three grand a week to host the gaming tables — would be her first step to becoming independent of Big Ron.

She may not have grown up in the church or anything, but she was tired of being a kept woman. She knew that's exactly what she was, no matter how much she'd tried to convince her younger self that she wasn't. Something deep inside of her was always telling her that it wasn't good for her to be living like that.

She went into her garage and slid her body into the hundred-grand Mercedes-Benz that Big Ron had bought for her six months ago. She had a special trip planned out today. She was on her way to Metro State Prison to visit her BFF, Carmen.

Lisa and Carmen had been friends ever since kindergarten. Unfortunately, Carmen's drug dealing boyfriend had tried to attack her seven years ago. Carmen had shot the fool in self defense. Somehow, she had been sentenced to ten years in lock-up on an attempted murder charge for her efforts.

Lisa frowned and shook her head. She hadn't had enough money back then to get her girl a decent defense attorney. She sure would've if she'd had it like that. But good defense attorneys ran into the tens of thousands of dollars.

An hour later, she was at the prison facility hugging her bestie.

"Hey, Carmen. You looking good, girl!"

Despite being on lock-down, Carmen gave her bestie a warm smile. "Hey, Lisa." She pointed at her designer outfit. "You looking good, too." Then she got to thinking of the first day of their senior year in high school all those years ago — the day when TIffany and her best friend, Angela, had made fun of Lisa's clothes, and Lisa had doled out a beatdown.

Despite herself, Carmen winked her eye. "I'm saved now, so I don't believe in glorifying violence. But I bet Angela and Tiffany wouldn't be making fun of you nowadays. You rocking Prada and Gucci. I bet you even have a few pair of red-bottoms."

Lisa smiled. She actually had several pair of the

thousand-dollar heels. "Yep. But I save my Christian Louboutins for special occasions."

"Next month's gonna be a special occasion for me. I told you the last time you visited that I had applied for early release due to good behavior—"

Lisa didn't let her girl finish speaking. She jumped up and gave her another hug. Then she pulled back and said, "You got it, didn't you?! They 'bout to spring you outta here!"

Carmen nodded her head. "I sure did. God blessed me, boo. Like I said...I'm gonna be walking outta this place the middle of next month."

Lisa sat back down with Carmen at the table. She sighed. "I just don't understand how you could stay committed to Jesus through all of this, Carmen. You served seven long years and all you were trying to do was defend yourself. You were trying to not become a statistic of domestic violence. You shot J-Dog in self defense."

Carmen nodded her head in understanding. "I can see where you're coming from, Lisa, but sometimes God works in mysterious ways. If I hadn't been locked up in this place, I never would've found God. It's because of my experience going through here that I finally broke down and cried out to him."

"You acting like you wouldn't give up the time that you spent in this joint."

Carmen shook her head. "Nope, I wouldn't. I was

living a foul lifestyle before I got in here. No telling how that would've ended for me." Her eyes met her bestie's. "That reminds me of you, boo. I know you have the nice clothes, the nice car, and you're living in a mini mansion, but the way you came about all of that stuff is suspect. It's the same way I had similar things before I got in here. God can give you an inner peace, a happiness that can surpass material items. I know you—," she patted her chest and looked Lisa in the eye. "I know right in here that you're not really feeling the life you're living. Before meeting Big Ron, you had big dreams for yourself. But him handing you everything on a silver platter in exchange for your company took away all of that. It took away your drive to go out into the world and be a go-getter. A *real* boss chick."

An hour later, Lisa had brought her visit with her girl, Carmen, to a close. As she hit the interstate and made her way over to her mama's house, she couldn't help but think about everything that Carmen had told her.

"I still have my dreams, Carmen," she whispered under her breath as she sped along the highway. "I just pushed them to the back burner for a little while. But they been coming back up in my mind lately. That's why I done started to distance myself from Big Ron."

It took her about thirty minutes to make it to her mom's place. Due to the money that Lisa had been getting from Big Ron, Lisa's mother and siblings no longer lived in the projects. Lisa had given her mother the funds to get herself a nice house on a decent side of town. Her mother even had a car now — which is something that she'd never had when Lisa had been growing up. Whenever they had wanted to go somewhere, they'd had to either walk, take the bus, or count on one of her momma's boyfriends taking them.

She pulled her Mercedes-Benz into the driveway of the modest-sized home located in a nicer side of town. Her ten-year-old sister, Alexis, pulled the door open before she could even ring the doorbell. "Hey, Lexi. where mama at?"

Alexis grinned. "She back there in her room watching TV. You taking me shopping this weekend, sis?"

"You know that's up to Mama, boo."

Alexis and Lisa's mother had been going to church lately. Now that she'd found Jesus, Diana was starting to turn down some of the money that Lisa had been giving her. She kept saying something about not wanting to keep letting dirty dollars into her life.

Lisa was pretty sure that her mama had thirty grand or so holed up in a safe somewhere in her house — which was leftovers from the money that she'd been giving her over the last five years.

Lisa humphed to herself. *I bet her ass ain't trying to come up off of them dollars of mine she been saving. I don't see her giving that away to charity or nothing. That's how she paying most of her bills around here.*

Lisa made her way to the back of the house and to her mother's bedroom. She knocked on the door and went inside when she said, "Come in."

"I'm just rolling through to see how you doing, mama. You need some money for anything? Alexis and them 'bout to go back to school. I was thinking about taking her and the other kids out with me shopping for clothes and whatnot."

Diana shook her head and frowned. Being complacent in the type of lifestyle her oldest child had been living for the past six or seven years was starting to get to her — especially now that she'd found Christ. "I don't want no more of your money from Big Ron or his casino, Lisa. I been getting along on what I been making from that side job I got and what little I was able to get from Shawn's daddy for child support."

"I know that child support check ain't nothing but about a hundred bucks per month, and you're only making five hundred dollars working part-time at Wally World. Your bills 'round here are way more than that. How the hell you gonna get along, Mama?"

"God got my back, Lisa. Your brother just got a job at Mickey D's. We gonna make it, you hear?"

"Well, at least let me take the kids shopping for back-to-school. After all, I *did* promise and I don't like breaking my promises to my little brothers and sisters. Family's all I got."

It was on the tip of Diane's tongue to say no. But

since she didn't want to break into her savings, she said okay instead. "This the last time though, Lisa," she warned.

Lisa nodded her head and gave her mother a hug. "Okay. I understand, mama."

After her oldest child had left her house, with a guilty heart, Diana said a quick prayer for her girl. She prayed that somehow, some way God would bring her out of the life she'd been living. "We both need your grace, Lord. Help my daughter to stumble into my prayer."

# CHAPTER 2

Two months later, Lisa had cut back on the number of hours that she was putting in at the casino. Instead of working thirty hours per week, she was now only doing twenty or so. She was spending most of her time researching her dream — which was opening a bakery.

"Well, what do you think about these, Shariece?"

Lisa's girl, Shariece, licked buttercream frosting off of her lips. She grinned and nodded her head. "I'd pay a dollar or two for one of 'em These here cupcakes are slamming, boo. I guess you really *are* good at this." She laughed. "I thought your ass was tryna be funny — you know, talking about you could cook real good and all."

Lisa smiled. "Well, I'm glad you like 'em. I'm starting to get some recipes ready for when I open up my bakery."

Shariece laughed. This was her first time hearing anything about any of that. "You?" she asked and

21

laughed again. "You gonna open a bakery, Lisa?"

"Yeah, girl. I decided to start squirreling some money away...starting next week. I'm gonna have me a nice place. I'm gonna specialize in cupcakes and cookies...basically desserts. It's gonna be called *The Real Sweet Spot*."

"The Real Sweet Spot?"

"Yeah." Lisa frowned. "Why you over there with that crazy smirk on your face?"

Shariece just chuckled, she didn't say a word.

"You think me opening up a bakery is funny, Shariece? Huh? That's what you think, boo?" Lisa pointed an accusatory finger at her girl and shook her head. "You just tasted my food...you said you liked it...that it was really good."

"It *was* good, boo...best cupcakes I had in a long time. And I really, really, really ain't trying to hate. I'm really not." Shariece laughed again. " It's just that I'm tryna imagine your ass with a legit gig. That's all. The last job I remember you having was back in high school at that bakery on First Street. And you quit there soon as you hooked up with Big Ron." She shook her head. "We ain't even gonna talk about you hosting tables over there at the casino, cause we both know that that little operation is all the way illegal...he paying you under the table. Big Ron is paying somebody a whole lotta hush money to keep that establishment open. He probably got the mayor and Lord knows who else under his thumb."

"What you're saying doesn't matter to me, Shariece Young. I know I can make this work. I know I can. That's all that really matters.

Smiling, Shariece snapped her fingers and began working her neck like only a Black girl knows how. "Well, I guess you just told my ass. I better leave that alone before I be feeling them hands of yours."

Lisa finally smiled. "You know I'm not like that anymore, boo. Getting into confrontations is for little girls, not grown ass women like myself." She paused for a few seconds then added. "But don't get it twisted though. I would definitely go to battle if I had to protect me and mine."

Shariece chuckled again. "I know that's right."

"Well, I'm about to roll on up outta here. Carmen just got outta prison yesterday. By now, she should be in that halfway house that they're making her live in for the next six months... You know as part of her probation."

"A'ight, boo. See you later."

*Thirty Minutes Later*:

Carmen had always told herself that when she got a little bit of money in her pocket, she was gonna help out the less fortunate. That she was going to do her part to make a difference. She may not have come about her money in the best of manners, but she was following through on her word. She was making good on her long ago promise to herself.

She made a quick stop at Ebenezer Christian Center — which was a church that always fed kids afterschool snacks and sandwiches, and it tutored them with their homework. Lisa had good memories of her and her siblings going there plenty of days when she'd been coming up. That center had been right on time for them a whole lot. It wasn't very often that Lisa's mother's foodstamp benefits would last the whole month. Especially the months when she'd have to sell her benefits at the local corner store and get only fifty cents for every dollar worth of stamps. Those were the months that Lisa and her younger siblings would get out of school and go home to nothing but mayonnaise sandwiches or something similar for dinner. She couldn't help but frown just from thinking about all of that.

She shook her head and forcibly pushed all of those thoughts aside. She dispelled those bad memories like dust on the wind. Then she pulled the money order for five hundred dollars out of her glove box. She nodded her head in satisfaction and proceeded to make her way towards the side of the church.

She came to a stop in front of a foot-long, mailbox-looking contraption that had been nailed onto the side of the building. The box read: *Donations*. She prompted dropped her contribution inside. Then she smiled. *That should help for a couple of weeks.*

As she turned around on her heel, a man approached the box with what looked like a check in his hand. Lisa told the fine, brown-skinned brotha good morning and she smiled — even though she didn't know him. Then she told him, "These people do a good job for the community. They need all the help they can get."

The man smiled back and told Lisa: "That's the God knows truth." Then he dropped his check into the box, just like she'd done with her money order.

That was the end of that little impromptu conversation. Ten minutes later, Lisa was standing in the foyer of a halfway house downtown — it was named *Halo House*. She gave her girl, Carmen, a warm hug.

"You don't know how good it is to finally be seeing you on the outside, Carmen. It just ain't been the same out here on these streets without my bestie."

Carmen and Lisa had been so tight growing up that Carmen felt the exact same way. She'd missed Lisa. She was smiling, but she also had the shine of tears of happiness in her eyes. "It's good to see you, too, girl."

Lisa nodded her head. "I gave you a whole day to get yourself settled into this place. Now… Are you ready to head out on the town or something to celebrate you being free? You know we have to have some type of celebration… Right?"

Carmen gave Lisa a look of warning. Then she said, "You know I'm saved, honey. So, I'm not interested in hitting up no clubs and partying like we used to. That's just not the way I roll anymore. And I have a curfew here at Halo House — all the residents do. I have to be back in by ten o'clock. Else the house matron is gonna report it to my probation officer." She frowned. "Truth be told, I kinda think that probation officer of mine is itching for some drama and a reason to get me locked back up." She shook her head. "But I don't intend on giving him the opportunity to do that."

"All right. I understand, boo. I wouldn't be taking any chances either — not if I was in your situation." Lisa smiled again. "The least you can do, though, is let me take your butt out to dinner. You can do that right there, can't you?"

"That sounds good to me. Honestly, girl, I been having a hankering for some good ol' fashioned soul food. You know they don't have nothing like that in lockup."

Lisa grinned. "Don't worry, boo. I got your back. I know the perfect place that we can hit up. You're gonna enjoy it."

Lisa frowned as she raked her eyes over Carmen's body. "But we probably need to take you to the mall to get you some decent clothes first." She smiled again. "I would say that you can borrow something of mine, but since you're saved and all, I think almost everything in my closet might just be a little bit too skanky or scandalous for your liking." She laughed at that and winked her eye. "Plus, we about the same size in the waist, but with them hips that your mama blessed you with, you gonna have all the men's eyes on the prize...they gonna wanna hit that thang from behind. I don't reckon a saved and sanctified woman is gonna wanna be drawing that type of attention... Huh?"

"Maybe some, but definitely not me."

Lisa chuckled. "I didn't think so. Go ahead and get your purse or whatever, Carmen. Let's go ahead and bounce."

Carmen had resisted at first, but she ended up agreeing to let Lisa purchase her an outfit or two. After she climbed into Lisa's Mercedes-Benz, Carmen looked over at her girl and said, "I know I been outta the loop for a while, but this is a hundred-grand vehicle, boo. Big Ron must really be making bank to put you into something like this."

Lisa nodded her head. "Yeah, he making bank all right. Like I told you a few years ago, he's not slinging dope out on the street anymore. He owns a casino. His joint caters to people with money...celebrities and whatnot." She backed out of the driveway and hit the road. Then she glanced over at her girl. "You told me that they were making you find a job as a condition of you living in that halfway house. How about I hook you up with Big Ron? You can host tables in his casino...just like I do. I be pulling in three grand per week. And I only work about twenty hours. I do two ten-hour shifts." She nodded her head. "As a favor to me — since you're my bestie and all — I'm sure I can sweet talk Big Ron into paying you the same thing."

Carmen frowned. "I don't like beating this over nobody's head and keep saying it, but I'm saved, Lisa. A casino ain't exactly the type of environment I need to be working in. Plus, I'm sure my parole officer wouldn't like it. And I'm pretty much sure that Big Ron is paying folks under the table."

Lisa nodded her head. "All of that is true, but maybe you can just work there for a little while.. You know, while you still looking for a regular job? At least you would be making good money. I know you broke. Ain't hardly nobody coming up out of prison with no money in their pocket." Lisa shrugged her shoulders. "At least you can come and take a look at the operation. You might just find that you like it."

Against her better judgment, Carmen nodded her head and said, "Okay. I guess it won't hurt to take a look."

"Good. We'll have dinner and then we'll roll on over and check it out."

# STUMBLING INTO A PRAYER

*Two and a Half Hours Later*:

Lisa pulled her Mercedes-Benz into a parking lot that was located behind a classy stuccoed building. The building was unassuming, but Carmen could tell that that it was nice. It had that type of Mediterranean style going for itself that a person would normally see somewhere like Rodeo Drive in California. It looked like the type of place that would cater to the rich and famous.

Lisa grinnned. "Well, Carmen...here we are." She unlocked her car doors. "Let's go ahead and get you inside so you can check everything out."

After going through what Carmen assumed was a security checkpoint, she followed Lisa down a short hallway. Everything had been quiet in the building up until the point that Lisa pulled open a set of expensive carved solid wood doors. Then they were hit in the face by the noise of people gambling and generally having a good time. It was like Vegas up in that joint.

Carmen looked around the casino and frowned. She'd known from the get-go that the gambling club wasn't gonna be the type of environment that she wanted to be working in. She was trying to live a saved lifestyle and everything that club represented was totally against that. Excessive drinking, drugging, swearing, and some of everything else under the sun...you name it, it was going on in that casino. *I want the money, but this isn't the environment for me, Lord.*

Lisa was grinning from ear to ear. She was right at home. As several slot machines sounded in the background, she asked Carmen, "What you think, boo?"

Carmen shook her head. "I can't do this, Lisa. Thanks but no thanks, honey."

Lisa was confused. She'd thought for sure that once she got her homegirl up in the club, she'd be changing her mind. "Are you sure, Carmen?"

Carmen nodded her head. "Yeah. I'm ready to go back to the halfway house... I'm ready to go back to Halo House."

"Well, can you hang around for a couple more hours? One of the girls who work the roulette table just went home sick. Big Ron wants me to take her place for a little while. Her replacement should be here in an an hour or so."

*This isn't the place for you, boo*, Carmen thought to herself. *Lisa got you up in here around a lot of mess.*

Carmen shook her head. "You don't have to take me back to the halfway house. I can find my way home. Okay?"

"Alright. See you later."

As she left the place on foot, Carmen said a prayer for her girl. She loved Lisa like a sister. She wanted God to move in and work his supernatural power in her life. *I want her to accept you into her heart and get herself saved, Lord.*

# STUMBLING INTO A PRAYER

When Lisa got herself situated behind the roulette table, Carmen had been gone for less than two minutes. It took only that long for all hell to break loose in the casino. Police officers and federal agents busted into the place with their guns ablazing. As an officer grabbed her from behind and slapped handcuffs on her wrists, Lisa knew she was in trouble. In the very back of her mind — in the place where she tended to file away things that she really wanted to ignore — in that place, she'd known that there was a possibility of this day coming.

*Me and Carmen about to switch positions. I'm in here working in an illegal operation... My ass about to be locked up.* She felt the cold metal of the handcuffs on her wrists. *Correction, I'm already locked up.*

She suspected her mama was finally gonna have to use that money that she'd given her years ago for this specific predicament. *My mama 'bout to have to bail me outta jail tonight. Ain't that messed up?*

# CHAPTER 3

The interrogation room downtown at the police station looked nothing like Lisa had imagined it would look. Not at all. In all the movies she'd ever seen, interrogation rooms were depicted as clean, sterile, light-filled places. This particular room that she was sitting alone in, it was dark and a little on the dingy side. She'd been waiting for going on an hour. Now she was starting to get impatient. "If they're gonna book me, they need to come on up in here and do it. The sooner they get it over with, the sooner I can be bailed out."

She heard the door opening behind her, but she didn't turn around.

"Ms. Washington... Right?"

She shook her head. She still didn't turn around to see the face of the man who was talking to her. "That's my name. You gonna book me or what?"

"Let's talk about what you were doing in that casino."

She finally turned around and looked straight into the face of the brotha who'd been depositing a check into the dropbox at Ebenezer Christian Center that morning.

"It's you," they both said at the same time. Then he added, "It's you...the anonymous donor who's been leaving five hundred bucks per month in the dropbox over at Ebenezer."

Nevermind that she was fearful of being arrested for the first time, Lisa got a little pissed off from the brotha asking about her donations. She frowned. "Since whoever was leaving that donation was supposed to be anonymous, how come you saying it's me who did it?"

"My father's the pastor over at Ebenezer. He's been the pastor there for the past twenty years. My mother started the program that you were donating to. She wanted to make sure that all the kids in the neighborhood were taken care off — that they had something decent to eat in the evenings — that they had tutoring available to give them a better shot in life—," he smiled, "—she's got a good heart like that. In the past few years, not too many people have been leaving donations in that box. But somebody's been leaving a five-hundred dollar money order in there every first Wednesday of the month for the past few years." He looked her in the eye and continued speaking. "Today was the first Wednesday of the month. There were only two donations in the dropbox today —

my mother's already told me that. Mine was one of them.
I saw you put something in there, too. So I know yours
was the second one." He nodded his head. "So yeah, I
pretty much know you're our anonymous donor."

Lisa knew when she'd been had — in other words,
she knew that the gig was up. She looked him in the eye
and said, "All right, but none of that has anything to do
with why I'm sitting up in here right now. Are you
arresting me or what? I need to move on with my life. If
you are, the sooner I make bail, the better. So I'd
appreciate it if you'd go ahead and get on with the get
on...you know, do whatever you gonna do."

"Like I said when I first stepped in here… What
were you doing in that casino, Miss Washington?"

"I was there visiting… A friend of mine had told me
about it, I wanted to see what all the hype was about."

"Is that right?"

She nodded her head. "Yeah, that's right."

He'd been briefed on the situation surrounding Lisa
Washington's arrest. According to the person who'd
handcuffed her that night, she'd been arrested under
suspicion that she was one of the operators or workers at
the illegal casino.

"You sure about that?" He asked.

She nodded her head again. "Yes, I'm sure."

He knew that she probably wasn't telling him the
truth, but the fact that she'd been anonymously donating
five-hundred dollars every month to feed the children in

their community touched his heart. *She's gotta be a good person, people don't do stuff like that if they're not.* He felt like he wanted to give her a break. *Maybe this will be a wake up call to her to get a different occupation... A wake-up call to turn her life around.*

Despite himself, he nodded his head. "All right, Ms. Washington. You were an uninformed guest there this evening...and not a participant in any of the activities. That's what I'm officially putting down on the books."

Lisa had been looking irritated, upset, and a little scared — ever since those handcuffs had been slapped on her wrists. Now she could barely believe what this brotha standing in front of her was telling her. Her eyes began to shine with excitement. "I can go now?"

He nodded his head. "Yeah. It's gonna take me about a half hour to get all your paperwork ready. But yeah. We're cutting you loose, Miss Washington." His eyes met hers. "Maybe this will be a wake-up call to you… A sign that God wants you in better surroundings. Know what I mean?"

She wasn't sure about all of that, but she was grateful to not be facing time in jail. Therefore, she nodded her head and said, "Yeah. I understand."

The following morning, Lisa showed up bright and early to pick Carmen up — she was supposed to be taking her on a job interview.

Carmen gave Lisa a hug as soon as she walked through the front door of Halo House. "Boo, I'm so glad to see your butt right now...you just don't know how glad I am. When I was walking away from the casino last night, I saw all the police rushing the building and arresting people. Then, when I was watching the news, they had a clip of them leading you out the building in handcuffs." She shook her head. "Girl, I was worried. I was praying for you, honey."

Lisa grinned. "You know I'm not a churchgoing type of sista, but I was praying for me, too. They took me downtown to the police station in handcuffs, but they ended up not arresting me. You ain't gonna believe it, girl... This fine ass detective came in and started questioning me. Then he decided to let me go — said he wasn't gonna press any charges."

A look of surprise came onto Carmen's face. "They didn't press any charges? Just like that?"

Lisa shook her head. "Nope...no charges are gonna be pressed against me. I know the detective knew my black ass was guilty of working in there, but he let me step on up out of that police station scot-free."

"Did you flirt with him or something? He let you walk? Just like that...I don't understand."

Lisa lifted her lips in a tiny smile. "Bruh-man sure was fine enough for me to wanna flirt with him, but naw, that ain't what happened. You see...he caught me slipping a five-hundred dollar donation into that deposit box down at Ebenezer Church yesterday morning. He don't know me from Adam, and I don't know him either, but we said hi to each other while we were at the dropbox. Then, when they arrested me last night, he was the detective who came into the interrogation room to question me — you know, to get my version of what I was doing down there. I told him I was just visiting. I know he knew I was lying, but he decided to cut me loose... Said something about how I should consider that a blessing. Said I should get up out of there and work on turning my life around."

Carmen nodded her head. Then she closed her eyes and held up one hand towards the heavens. "Glory!" she shouted. "Glory, glory, glory!" She looked her girl dead in the eye. "You just received a blessing, Lisa. God allowed you and that detective to meet up yesterday morning at that dropbox. Then he sent him in that room to question you... If anybody else had stepped up in there, things definitely wouldn't have turned out the way they did. You really *should* be thanking God for this blessing. And you really *should* consider turning your life around."

Carmen shook her head and continued speaking. "I'm pretty much sure you would've been about to do some hard time if God hadn't shown you this little act of mercy, boo. I've been praying for you, girl. I've been praying something fierce."

Lisa didn't really know what to say to all of that. "Uh...um... Okay, thanks."

As soon as she'd dropped Carmen back off at Halo House from her job interview, Lisa decided to make her way back home. She'd only been in the house that Big Ron had bought for her five minutes when she heard someone ring her doorbell. She checked the security system video camera and saw that it was Big Ron's alpha chick, Alizay, standing out there.

Lisa didn't have any beef with Alizay, so she pulled open her front door, smiled at the girl and said, "Why you rolling up in here visiting me this morning, boo?"

Alizay frowned. "You and me always been cool, so I came to give you a heads up, Lisa. The feds are gonna be busting up in here... They taking all the properties that Big Ron owns tomorrow morning. Apparently, they're not just holding him on racketeering charges. They been investigating. They holding him on charges for some murders he committed back when he was slinging dope. A cop that Big Ron has on his payroll downtown told me about everything. If you don't wanna go to prison, you gonna want to have yourself and all your shit up out of here... And I'm talking like by today."

Lisa didn't like hearing that, but she thanked Alizay for the heads up. After the girl had left the mini mansion that Lisa was living in, Lisa frowned and flopped down on her five thousand dollar pure white sofa. *Where the hell am I gonna go now? This here house is in Big Ron's name.*

She shook her head in disbelief. *At least I convinced him to buy the Benz in my name. At least I still own something.*

She sat there contemplating everything for five minutes or so. Then she stood up. She had a game plan. She was going to go over to McKinley High and pick up her brother, Jerome. Then she planned on them going to get a U-Haul truck and signing up for some storage space somewhere. *I got some expensive furniture up in here. Oh they can have the house, but they not gonna have my things. You can trust and believe that.*

*The Following Morning*:

Living in her mama's house again felt weird to Lisa. But she hadn't had anywhere else to go, so she hadn't had a choice. Her valuables were on lockdown in a self-storage center. As for herself, she was now laying in bed in her mama's guest room.

She loved her mama, but she really didn't feel like talking to her that morning. So, Lisa got up and made her way out the house.

Over the years, she'd developed a love for Starbucks' mocha frappuccinos. With thoughts of getting her favorite coffee drink into her belly, she pointed her car in the direction of the mall. She preferred the ambiance in there to any other Starbucks in the city. Unfortunately, other people felt the exact same way — that's why seating was always tight in that particular Starbucks location. It was no different this morning when Lisa snagged herself a seat. She'd only been sipping on her brew a couple of minutes when a deep masculine voice said, "Mind if I sit down at this empty chair at your table?"

The tables were bistro style, so they only sat two people. Lisa didn't particularly feel like sharing her table with a stranger that morning. When she looked up into the face of the person who'd just spoken to her, she realized that it wasn't a stranger at all — not really. It was the detective who'd allowed her to walk free from jail the other day.

She smiled at him because he was smiling at her. Then she waved her hand and said, "I'm not used to sitting around with the law, but sure. Knock yourself out, detective."

"Thanks."

He proceeded to pull the chair out and sat down. "What have you been doing with yourself for the past two days, Miss Washington?"

She looked up. "Not much. But before we continue

on with this little conversation, I'm gonna let you know that I think it's unfair that you know my name but I don't know yours."

He smiled again. "That's right, we weren't really formally introduced, were we?" He reached out his palm towards her. "Jason Mathis. And it's a pleasure to meet you."

She had a look of doubt all in her eyes. She was thinking about what had happened downtown at the police station. "Really? It's a pleasure to meet me? I can't imagine that being the case — especially given the circumstances that we really met under."

"Personally, I think we met under really good circumstances. We were both making financial contributions to a very worthy cause."

Lisa had forgotten all about that. She'd forgotten that technically, they'd met at Ebenezer Church at the dropbox. Thinking about that made her frown. She wouldn't be able to give any more five-hundred dollar donations to the church's afterschool program. She was disappointed about that.

"What's wrong, Ms. Washington?"

"Just thinking about something… That's all."

Jason wasn't a fool — he'd looked deeper into the specifics of the case that she'd been involved in. He knew all about her involvement with Big Ron, and he also knew that she was probably now broke and destitute. He felt kind of sorry for her. *Even though I probably shouldn't be feeling that way. She chose to align herself with a con man, a criminal.* Despite him thinking that to himself, there was something about Lisa Washington that seemed good and decent to him.

"You've been donating to the church, but we've never seen your face up in there on Sunday morning. How about you come on over and see what we're all about?"

*Is everybody I run into gonna be trying to get my ass saved now? First it started with my bestie — it started with Carmen. Then my mama jumped on board the Jesus train. Now this fool is sitting across from me looking up in my face offering invitations to his church. What in the world is going on? What's up with all of that?*

Lisa didn't have any more time to ponder on what was on her mind because someone approached their little table and said, "Hey, Jason."

Lisa looked up into the face of none other than her arch nemesis from high school — the girl who had made it her business to continuously try to pick on her. The girl that she had popped in the mouth and gotten suspended behind on the very first day of her senior year. It was nobody but Tiffany Scott.

Tiffany realized the identity of the woman sitting with Jason the second that Lisa realized that it was her. A nasty look came onto Tiffany's face, which only lasted a second or so. Why? Well, Tiffany liked Jason — she had a big crush on him. She wasn't interested in him seeing her looking unpleasant.

Tiffany turned her lips up in a fake smile. "Hi, Lisa. I haven't seen you in ages." She looked at Jason, then back at Lisa, then back at Jason again. "The two of you know each other?"

Jason smiled at Tiffany. Then he smiled at Lisa. He nodded his head. "I guess you could say that."

Keeping with the fakeness, Tiffany grinned. "Oh, for real? Where y'all know each other from?" She laughed. "I know it's not from church. Church's not exactly your thing, is it, Lisa?"

Tiffany didn't wait for Lisa to answer, she continued speaking. "And I know it's not from the club, cause Jason's saved. He wouldn't be caught up in there. Maybe he was arresting you or something." she laughed. "Just kidding about that. Seriously though, how did the two of you meet?"

Lisa really didn't feel like dealing with Tiffany and all her fakeness and pettiness.

She frowned and stood up. She slung her Coach bag over her shoulder and took her coffee drink into her hand. She directed her words toward Detective Mathis when she said, "I'm gonna have to pass on your invitation to Ebenezer Christian Center... But thanks for the invite though. Enjoy the rest of your morning,... Okay?"

He smiled at Lisa. "You, too."

Lisa didn't say a word to Tiffany. On account of not wanting to be rude — despite the fact that she knew that's exactly what Tiffany deserved — she nodded her head in the girl's direction and walked away. *I feel sorry for Detective Mathis if he ends up hooking up with that bougie fake ass trick...real sorry.*

Normally, Lisa would've taken herself on a mini shopping spree — seeing that she was already in the mall and all. But given her new financial situation, meaning that she was broke, she knew better than trying anything like that. She slowly made her way past some of her favorite stores without even going inside. When she finally got into her car, she sat behind the wheel and started reflecting on everything. She really was worried about what she was gonna do next. She'd graduated from high school, but like her girl, Shariece, had kidded about a few weeks ago, she hadn't worked a real job since her part-time gig at the bakery back in the twelfth grade.

She shook her head. *That was almost eight years ago. I don't have any experience in doing nothing — besides sitting around and looking pretty. Ain't nobody gonna hire my ass.*

When Jason Mathis came out of the mall and walked up to the SUV that was parked beside Lisa's vehicle, she was still contemplating on everything. She didn't feel like drawing any attention to herself, so she didn't say a word to him —not even a wave of her hand. When she noticed a look of irritation on his handsome face and noticed him throw his hands up in the air in disbelief, she realized that he'd most likely locked his keys in his vehicle. When she peeped him whipping his cell phone out his back pocket, she got out of her car. Before he could dial whatever number he was trying to call, she said, "You locked out... Huh?"

He frowned and nodded his head. "Yeah. First time it's ever happened, too. I don't have one of those number keypads on my car door to get myself in manually. I'm gonna have to call triple A. I think they only charge twenty-five bucks or something similar to get me in. At least that's what I think they're website said when I signed up with them almost five years ago."

Lisa shook her head. "Don't call them. I think I can help you out. It'll be quicker and cheaper...in fact, it'll be free. Give me a few seconds. I'll be right back."

She went back to her car and rummaged inside her Coach bag for the three-foot-long piece of string that she always kept in there. Then she came back over to where Jason was standing.

She quickly fashioned the length of string into a slipknot. She flashed him a smile. "It'll probably take me about five minutes, but I can get you into your ride."

Four minutes later, Detective Mathis was looking on in disbelief as Lisa lowered the slipknot into his car and tightened it around the stem of his car lock. She pulled the string tight, then opened the door for him. She smiled and said, "Here you go, Jason. Like I told you back in

Starbucks: *Have yourself a good day*."

He couldn't help but grin at her retreating back. "Thanks, Ms. Washington."

As she slowly backed out of her parking spot, Lisa was grinning, too. Then she stopped and rolled down her window. She said, "Just in case we happen to ever run into each other again — which I really doubt since Atlanta's such a big city — but just in case we do, how about just calling me Lisa. Miss Washington's my mama's name. It makes me feel old."

He nodded his head. "All right, *Lisa*." He'd intentionally placed emphasis on her birth name. "Enjoy your day."

"You, too, Jason."

She'd been living in her mama's house for less than twenty-four hours and Lisa thought that it was ironic that her mom was already sending her on errands. While she'd been in the middle of unlocking Jason Mathis' car door for him, she'd gotten a text from her mama asking her to pick up a gallon of milk from the grocery store. Lisa really felt like going straight home to her new bedroom and reflecting on her current situation, but since she didn't feel like getting on her mother's bad side, she took herself right to the Super Walmart. She hadn't even gotten out of her car when Jason parked his SUV right beside her Benz.

She got out of her vehicle at about the same time that Jason got out of his. She flashed him a smile. "You're not following me, are you, Jason?"

He laughed. He shook his head. "Nope. Friday generally starts my weekend. I'm off most Fridays, Saturdays, and Sundays. Friday is my normal grocery shopping day. Wally World has some of the best prices around... So here I am."

He winked his eye at her. "Just in case you're wondering, back there in the mall after you left, I never did tell Tiffany how you and I met."

It wouldn't have rocked Lisa's world if he'd said something to Tiffany, but all the same, Lisa was happy that he hadn't told the girl that the two of them had met while she'd been arrested — detained really and being held for questioning. Thanks to Jason, she never was officially booked.

She gave him a rueful little smile. "Was it that obvious that there's no love lost between me and Tiffany Scott?"

He smiled, too. "Pretty much so."

Lisa couldn't help but think how Tiffany had been in the mall bragging about how her and Jason went to the same church together. Suddenly, it seemed like a good idea to Lisa to show up in Ebenezer Christian Center as Jason's special guest. *Which in my eyes, essentially means that I'll be his date. Petty as Tiffany is, she gonna be thinking the same thing too...that I'm his date.*

"I was thinking about that invitation that you gave me to go to church, Jason... You know, on my drive over here. Truth be told, I haven't been inside a church building in years — almost a decade. I'm nervous about going. If I could go with a friend, that would make it easier on me. You wouldn't happen to be open to being my escort this Sunday—," she gave him a charming smile, "—would you?"

Jason was all for bringing souls to Christ. His grin widened by almost a hundred percent. He nodded his head. "Give me your address. I'll pick you up at ten thirty Sunday morning."

As Lisa walked out of the Walmart with the gallon of milk that her mom had asked for, she was grinning from ear to ear. *I can't wait to see the look on that bougie trick's face when I walk up in her church with the man she's so obviously crushing on. Shoot, I'm gonna see if I can get him to take me out to dinner, too. Probably even on some more dates somewhere. That should really piss her off right there.*

Lisa frowned and shook her head. *She was back there in the mall being all nice-nasty toward me. That shit was uncalled for. It's time for me to dole out a little payback... Payback for right now, and payback for ol' time sake.*

# *C*HAPTER 4

Now that her girl, Carmen, was out of prison, Lisa had every intention of spending some good quality time with her. Lisa rolled up on the halfway house that Carmen was living in the following morning. Since they'd made plans to hit up the IHOP together, Carmen was waiting for Lisa out there on the front porch.

They had made it to IHOP and were tucking into their grand slam breakfasts when Lisa began telling Carmen about her little run-in with Tiffany.

Carmen shook her head. "I woulda thought that she would've done more growing up than that. High school was almost ten years ago. Talking to you like that in front of that detective dude was just plain petty." Carmen was smiling, but half-serious when she asked, "You didn't pop her in the mouth again, did you, boo?"

Lisa shook her head. She smiled. "Naw. I was tempted. But to tell you the truth, I consider myself to be a little bit too classy for acting like that now. That's not how a real lady carries herself — fighting out in the

49

streets and whatnot. There's other ways to do battle with tricks like Tiffany Scott."

A knowing look came into Carmen's eyes. "Oh, Lord. I may not have gotten to see you too often over the last eight years because I was in prison, but I know that look on your face. What you done did? Or better yet, what are you planning on doing?"

Lisa placed a fake look of offense on her face. "Me? Little ol' me? What are you talking about, honey?"

"I know you're planning something, Lisa. You and I been knowing each other since before kindergarten. I know you, girl. Now talk. Go ahead and spill it."

Lisa smiled. "A'ight, a'ight... Since I obviously can't get nothing past your nosy — naw, I'm not gonna say nosy, I'm gonna say observant. Now like I was saying, since I can't get anything past your observant little behind, I'll tell you about my plan."

"Good… Somebody needs to be keeping you out of trouble."

Lisa laughed at that. Then she said, "For real though, it appears that Tiffany has a crush on Detective Mathis — I picked up on that when she was trying to bust on me at the Starbucks the other day. Well, he'd invited me to his church while we were having our coffee. I had told him that I wasn't interested — I know you know I don't be up in nobody's church like that. Then I got to thinking about everything, and when I ran into him at Wally World day before yesterday, I told him that I would be happy to go if he took me."

Lisa lifted her lips in a smile. "I can't wait to see the look on Tiffany's face when she sees me roll up into that church on Detective Mathis' arm." She looked Carmen in the eye. "You on fire for Jesus, you should come along, too. That way you can take a picture of Tiffany's face for me. I'll have one for my memory book."

Carmen hadn't decided on what church she was going to go to now that she was back on the outside, so showing up at Ebenezer Christian Center seemed like a good enough idea to her.

"A'ight, Lisa. I think I'll take you up on that offer… But not so I can take snapshots of Tiffany. I'm going because I'm ready to get my praise on."

Carmen had really wanted to tell Lisa that she didn't think that what she was doing was a good idea, but she held her tongue on that. *Who knows, this might just be God's way of getting my girl up in the church. He might just have a special message planned for Lisa this Sunday. God works in mysterious ways. We'll just have to wait and see what happens tomorrow.*

Lisa didn't have any dresses in her closet that were church appropriate, but she did own a Gucci two-piece suit. She'd been hesitant about wearing pants to church — from the last she remembered, only skirts and dresses were allowed in church on women. When she'd asked Carmen about it, Carmen had told her that nowadays, some women were wearing pants to service. Lisa had been happy to hear about that, because she hadn't wanted to go spend any money on any clothes. It's not like she had a job or anything just yet — even though she'd finally wrapped her brain around the fact that it was time for her to start looking for one...well past time.

Wearing a house robe, Lisa's mama, Diana, knocked on the guest bedroom door and walked in. "You need to be getting yourself up and dressed so that you can head on over to the church with me and the kids this morning, Lisa. That's what you need to be doing."

Lisa hadn't told her mama about her plans yet, so she really couldn't wait to see the look on her mother's face when she made her big announcement. "I'm going to church today, mama. I'm just not going to *your* church. I'm heading over to Ebenezer Christian Center. You remember them, don't you? They the ones with the afterschool program that we used to eat at...back when I was at McKinley High."

A look of disbelief came on Diana's face, followed by one of approval. "You're going to church, Lisa? For real? You ain't joking about that?"

Lisa pointed at the clothes that she'd laid out on the guestroom bed. "Yep. I'm going to church all right. I got my clothes picked out already. I didn't wanna show up in the house of the Lord looking like I just stepped out of some club, so I had to go with a pantsuit as my best option. But I'm gonna be up in there."

"Praise, Jesus! Praise, Jesus!" Diana gave her daughter a hug. "You don't know how long I've been praying that you'd finally decide to take yourself up into somebody's house of worship. I guess it took the Lord shutting down that casino and taking Big Ron's money away from you for you to finally realize that you needed Jesus in your life."

Lisa hadn't been counting on it, but she realized right then and there that allowing her mother to think that she was running to God would make her life a whole lot easier while she was living under her mama's roof. *I'mma have to play this for all that it's worth. Maybe going to church every Sunday won't be too bad of a thing. It ain't like I got anything better to do anyway.*

*What are you doing?*

That's the question that Lisa had wanted to ask Jason when he walked with her from her mama's front door and to the passenger side of his SUV. Then she realized exactly what he was doing — he was opening the car door for her.

She'd never had a man do anything like that when picking her up to go anywhere. She'd dated Big Ron for years. If her car door got opened, it was because she'd done it herself. But she wasn't gonna lie. She liked the extra attention.

The man who was taking her to church that day looked good and smelled good — Jason was close to six feet tall with the body of a bodybuilder and the face of a male model — so she really wouldn't have minded if they had been out on a real date. But she already knew that something like that wasn't gonna happen — them going on a date. *Jason Mathis ain't the type of brotha who'd be checking for a round-the-way, everyday chick like myself. I'm fabulous and all, but I'm not his type. And he probably ain't even mine either.*

After he'd gotten into the driver seat, Jason smiled. "You're gonna enjoy services today, Lisa. I just know you are."

"Yeah… All right." She had agreed with him, but she wasn't feeling it. She was just saying something to be saying something. She really felt like getting along with Jason and she figured that being agreeable would be the best approach to reaching that goal.

He turned his lips up in a smile. "You don't really believe me, do you? You don't think you're gonna have a good time at church today, do you?"

Lisa shrugged her shoulders. "Real talk, I don't really know. But I'mma go on what you're saying. If you think I'm gonna have a good time, then I might just be about to have a good time."

"Well, at least you have an open mind about it. That's

what's important. When we come to God, he accepts us all as we are and gives us the opportunity to grow and develop into his likeness. You don't have to be perfect just starting out. I've been going to church for most of my life. It's something that I'm definitely not — perfect that is. I have my faults."

*I bet you don't have more than me, church boy*, she thought to herself. She knew she was far from perfect, but to the most part, she tried to do right by people.

He winked his eye. "And before we get to the church, I wanna let you know that you look stunning in that little get up. It's very appropriate for church. When I was growing up, women didn't wear pantsuits in the sanctuary, but they do it all the time now. Especially at Ebenezer."

She smiled. "How'd you know I was having my doubts about it?"

He grinned, too. "I don't for sure know how I knew. I just kinda felt it."

Ten minutes later, they were walking into the main atrium of Ebenezer Christian Center together. Then Jason placed his hand under her elbow and escorted her into the sanctuary. It brought Lisa untold amounts of pleasure to witness Tiffany shooting daggers of jealousy and anger at her with her eyes.

*That's what I'm talking about right there*, Lisa thought to herself as she flashed the girl a smile. She didn't get a pleasant look back in return — oh no, quite the opposite. But it's not like Lisa wasn't expecting that. She was kind of tickled to see Tiffany's reaction.

Carmen was already seated, so she waved her hand, beckoning Lisa to come over and sit beside herself and Janelle — Janelle was an ex-felon who was trying to turn her life around, who lived in the same halfway house as Carmen.

Lisa and Jason made their way over to Carmen and claimed two seats beside her. Then a few minutes later, the service really got into full swing with praise and worship.

Lisa was pleasantly surprised that to the most part, she enjoyed the service. The choir could really blow — there was nothing to not enjoy about that. And for a few seconds, she actually thought that she had felt something, a tingling that went all throughout her body. She was surprised by that and in denial about it, too. So, by the end of the service, she decided to just chalk it up to nerves. However, she couldn't get the pastor's sermon out of her head. The message that the preacher had delivered had moved her. He'd talked about God having a call on every individual's life. He'd said that some people chose to ignore that call...for whatever reason. He'd insisted that it was time for everybody who'd been sitting in that church building that day to answer that call from God.

Growing up, from time to time, Lisa had always felt like there was a little voice in her head telling her to do right — that's why she always tried her hardest to treat everybody she knew decent. She'd never really equated that voice to actually being the voice of God. But now she was starting to wonder about that. She was interested in learning more about it. The pastor had mentioned that he would be doing a part two of his sermon the following Sunday, and Lisa had every intention of showing up. *There might just be something to church after all. I don't know. But maybe I'm about to find out.*

After the service was over with and everybody was filing out of the church, Lisa noticed Tiffany rolling her eyes at her. It felt good to her to witness that. After the way Tiffany had treated her, Lisa felt like Tiffany deserved to be pissed off.

Lisa was happy that Jason once again had his hand tucked under her elbow as he escorted her out of the church. She made a mental note to actually attend the Bible study that was going to be held the following Wednesday. She figured that she could nonchalantly drop the news to somebody sitting in there that she and Jason had gone out to dinner after church. Lisa smiled to herself. *Jason taking me out to dinner should really get Tiffany ass aggravated. I like that.*

Since Carmen and Janelle had taken the bus to church that morning, Lisa decided to get Jason to drop her bestie and her friend, Janelle, off at Halo House. After that little detour, the couple continued on to an early after church dinner at one of Lisa's favorite restaurants — Red Sizzler, where the food was stupid delicious but tended to run on the lower end of the pricey side of the cost spectrum. Lisa had thought nothing about dropping forty bucks per person on a meal while she was working at the casino for Big Ron. Now she cringed at the idea of spending six bucks at Mickey D's.

She glanced over at Jason as he sped along the highway. "You sure you wanna go to Red Sizzler? Plates be averaging forty bucks there."

Jason nodded his head and smiled. "I know how much it costs. I've been there a few times on special occasions. But thanks for your concern though. That's mighty thoughtful of you."

"You taking me out to lunch slash dinner isn't a special occasion, Jason. This isn't even a real date or anything. And you just met me day before yesterday."

"I beg to differ, Lisa. It *is* a special occasion. God told me that in my spirit while we were in church today. You felt something… You felt HIM. Not only did you feel God, but you opened your mind and your heart up to him a little. That was the first step, and you took it. I think that definitely calls for a celebration." He smiled. "A forty-dollar per plate one."

She glanced over at him with doubt in her eyes. "God told you all of that while we were in church?"

He nodded his head. "Yep. He sure did."

As much as she wanted to, Lisa found that hard to believe. But based on the look on Jason's face, she could tell that he did indeed believe in what he'd said to her. Then she got to thinking about that tingling that she'd felt in her body during praise and worship...that overwhelming sensation of joy and peace.

It had only lasted for a few seconds and she had ended up convincing herself that it was just nerves, but now she was really starting to wonder about that. *Is that what he's talking about?* She asked herself. Something instinctively told her that it was. But she wasn't ready to admit that yet, so she skillfully moved the discussion over to a different topic...the weather.

Lisa couldn't stop laughing at the joke that Jason had just told her. She grinned at him and said, "Coming from where I come from, we tend to not like five-o. But I'mma have to make an exception in your case. You cool, Detective Jason Mathis. I like you."

He laughed. "Thanks...I think. And for the record, you're cool, too, Lisa. I have to admit that I've enjoyed my day with you. All of it."

She could tell that he was telling the truth and that made her feel good on the inside. There was an easy-going type of vibe between her and Jason Mathis. She didn't understand it, but she wasn't gonna fight it. She intended on going with the flow. *Going out on a few dates with him to piss Tiffany off is gonna be fun. I'm sure I can get him to agree to take me out somewhere again. I just know it.*

She was suddenly interested in learning more about him. "I always wondered what would make a brotha wanna become a police officer. What made you go down that career path, Jason?"

He thought about her question for only about a half second, then he said, "I just always really liked the idea of protecting and serving my community. Growing up in Black America, I had always heard about how there needed to be more police officers of color. Unfortunately, racial profiling by law enforcement officers is a real thing." He shook his head and continued speaking. "So I figured I could do my part to actually do something about it. Be part of the solution, instead of part of the problem. I like to think to myself that by me holding the police officer position that I do, it means that there's one less person who's a neo-Nazi or skinhead on the force. I put Christ first any case I'm involved in. I allow him to talk to me and through me, and then I act accordingly."

Her eyes met his. "Like you did for me last week... Huh? I could've been sitting somewhere in a jail cell right now instead of eating this delicious meal with you, but I'm not. And I have you to thank for that."

"God had his hand over the situation, Lisa. He put it in my spirit that you're a good person and that he wants to use you for good." He shook his head. "It wasn't like I could turn my back on that — even though I suspected that the story you were spinning me wasn't exactly legit."

A feeling of guilt settled over her. "You knew, didn't you?"

"That you were doing more than visiting that casino?" He nodded his head. "Yeah...I knew all right. I was pretty much sure of it. Especially since your name's in Big Ron's file as his girlfriend."

She felt a heated blush of embarrassment in her cheeks in response to him saying that. She hadn't talked to Big Ron since that night and she really didn't feel like doing so ever again. She grimaced. "Big Ron's in my past... And not just because he's going to prison. We had other conflicts between us. A breakup was gonna happen soon either way." She looked him in the eye. "I'm just glad that you didn't lock me up...even though you knew the truth."

"God put it in my spirit not to."

"Well, I guess I need to be giving God some thanks."

"Yeah. That would be a good idea. That's definitely what I'd do if I were in your situation."

*Later on that Night*:

Jason said his prayers and laid out his work clothes for the following day. Then he got into bed. As he closed his eyes and prepared himself for falling asleep for the evening, his mind began an automatic playback of his day. Lisa Washington was the star of the mental video that was playing in his brain. He smiled just from thinking about her. Then he felt a sensation of thankfulness when he recalled her mentioning that she was no longer with Big Ron. He didn't exactly understand why he should've been so excited about that.

He squinted his eyes together for a few seconds. Then he nodded his head. *I'm excited because it means that she won't have that negative influence in her life...that'll free her up for more time for a relationship with God. That's all there is to it. Nothing more nothing less.*

He totally ignored the little voice in his head that said: *Yeah, right. Keep trying to convince yourself of that, bruh. You know you kinda like that girl. You just glad that she a free agent.*

*Across Town at Lisa's Mama's House*:

Lisa snuggled under the covers in her mother's guest room. Then she closed her eyes and did something that she hadn't done in a very long time — ever since she'd been a little girl really. She began to talk to God. "If you're real like Jason, Carmen, and my mama say you are, then show yourself to me, God. I want to feel your presence in my life. Let me know that you exist. You, Jesus, the Holy Ghost...I'm checking for any and all of y'all."

She suddenly felt that same tingly feeling run through her body — the one that she'd felt in church earlier that day. *Maybe you are real, God, but I'm stubborn. I'mma need a little bit more proof than that. I'll follow you if I know for sure that you're there. I'll become your number one fan.*

# CHAPTER 5

Looking for a job was a frustrating thing for Lisa. She was putting in applications left and right — even at a few places that she knew weren't gonna hire her because she didn't exactly have all of the qualifications, but she was close to having them. Like the bakery she'd just walked out of for instance. She had all the skills they were looking for, seeing that she'd been practicing baking at home for years, but she didn't have the two-years of verifiable on-the-job experience that they wanted her to have — although she'd worked in a bakery for a year back in highschool.

*This is gonna be a whoooole lot harder than I thought*, she said in her brain as she climbed into her Benz and drove off.

Then she got to thinking about all of her stuff that she had locked up in a self storage unit on the outskirts of town. She had some expensive items in that thing. Designer furniture and whatnot. Her refrigerator had costed five grand new, and her stove had been two grand. Lisa had taken all of those items out of the house Big Ron had had her in. Not to mention the designer clothes she had in storage. She took comfort in the fact that she knew she could pawn all of that, or sell it online at Craigslist or somewhere similar.

She began mentally deciding on what she would let go of to get a cool grand in her pocket. Since she was living rent-free with her mama right now, she figured that a thousand dollars would last her at least two good months — *maybe even three if I don't do anything crazy with the cash.*

She pushed all thoughts on that particular little subject out her mind. Then she began thinking about her plans for the rest of the day. It was Wednesday, so she intended on going to Ebenezer Christian Center for their Bible study — just so she could rub her after-church dinner with Jason in Tiffany's face. The session would be starting at six o'clock that evening. Seeing that it was only a little past one in the afternoon, she had plenty of time to get ready for that.

As she hit the interstate, she began thinking about Jason. She'd been thinking about him off and on since she'd last seen him three days ago. She'd been thinking about God, too — more specifically, about how she wanted him to move in her life. She'd been talking to him every day, asking him to show her that he did indeed exist. She hadn't heard anything back as of yet, so she was beginning to get a little bit frustrated.

*How come other people can feel you and know you're there, but I can't?* That's what she asked herself as she changed lanes on the interstate.

After she'd thought that, a freakish thing happened. A once in a billion type of thing. A big chunk of cement broke loose from the overpass that she'd just driven under and missed her car by a mere inch or so. Her heart was beating at the rate of a mile per minute as she looked in her rearview mirror at that refrigerator-sized chunk of cement bumping along the shoulder of the interstate. *Was that you, God?* She asked herself. *Was that you protecting me? Was that you showing me that you're there? You showing me your strength and power?*

A tiny voice in her head told her yes. For the first time ever, she was starting to believe in that higher power that she'd heard other people talking about. She didn't want to seem greedy, but she wanted more.

Maybe I'll get something out of this Bible study session today. We'll just have to wait and see.

Not wanting to go to Bible study alone, Lisa picked Carmen and Janelle up from Halo House and took them with her. Lisa didn't know Janelle very well, but since Carmen liked the girl and saw her as a friend, Lisa decided to be cool with her. She wasn't gonna lie though, it seemed weird to Lisa that her born-again bestie would accept someone who was obviously a lesbian as a friend. Everything that Lisa had ever heard about Christianity pointed towards most of them disliking gays — well at least with Lisa's limited knowledge she thought they did.

She smiled at both Carmen and Janelle as they got into her car. Janelle climbed into the back seat and Lisa looked in her rearview mirror at the girl and said, "I know you came to church with me on Sunday, but I wouldn't have figured that churching was your thing, Janelle. You're obviously gay — you're butch — and I didn't think that church folk like people who live that type of lifestyle." Then she added, "And I ain't trying to bust on you or nothing. It's just that I'm not fake. I keep it real with everybody I deal with. I keep it one hundred."

Janelle smiled at Lisa. "You cool with me, boo. I ain't got no time for fake ass niggas anyway. I'll take somebody who speaks their mind like yourself over fakers. Now to answer your question, I grew up in the church. I was locked up for fifteen years for shooting and killing my abusive husband. I just got out two months ago." She frowned. "Keeping it real, I got mad at God over that...over me being imprisoned and all. I met this lesbo in lockup and she turned me out. I been with women ever since, and I ain't looked back. But I been kinda feeling like God's been talking to me lately. So I decided to lend him an ear for a little bit… You know, see what He talking about."

Janelle nodded her head. Then she said, "Since we on the subject, and we keeping it real and all, it don't exactly seem like you're the church type either, Lisa. What's your story?"

Lisa didn't really have any shame in her game. She told Janelle everything.

Janelle chuckled. "Wait a minute? You just rolling up in church cause you wanna make some trick mad? That's your only reason?"

Lisa nodded her head. "Pretty much so. The funny thing is though, I think God is talking to me or some shit. I was up in service on Sunday and I felt this warm feeling all over me and this tingling from the top of my head down to the toes of my feet."

Carmen, who'd been quiet up until now, smiled. Then she began clapping her hands and saying "Glory!". "That was him, boo. That was God. You felt him, Lisa. That was the Holy Spirit you were feeling." Happy, Carmen nodded her head. "I've been praying for you, girl. It seems like those prayers are starting to work."

Lisa halfway believed her bestie. Especially after what had happened out on the interstate with that chunk of cement. Her mama had been watching the local afternoon news that day and Carmen had seen that there was a handful of people in critical condition in the hospital over that highway incident.

*I think you might just be real, God*, she thought to herself. *I'm starting to think that there's no other explanation for everything that's been going on with me lately. From you keeping me outta prison behind that casino mess, to you keeping me safe out there on the interstate today. I coulda lost my life, that chunk of cement was only inches from crushing my car. But I didn't die out there...I was able to drive away free and clear.*

Carmen reached across the center console and gave Lisa's hand a loving, excited squeeze. "You felt Him, boo."

Lisa smiled. "Yeah. I think I felt Him."

Despite the fact that she thought that she was starting to feel God move in her life, Lisa still had every intention of following through with her plan of pissing Tiffany off. Lisa paid close attention during Bible study and even learned a thing or two. Then, when everything was over with, she decided to move her focus off of Jesus and put her little plan involving Tiffany into high gear. Before she could do that though, a middle-aged woman who looked vaguely familiar came over to her and gave her a hug.

"Welcome to Ebenezer Christian Center, baby. You said your name was Lisa when you introduced yourself at the beginning of Bible study... Right?"

Lisa smiled and nodded her head. "Yes, my name's

Lisa Washington."

"I'm Eleanor Mathis. Now, I remember why your face seems so familiar. You and your little brothers and sisters used to come over here for tutoring and afternoon snacks. It had to have been almost ten years ago."

Lisa realized at that moment that that's why Eleanor had looked so familiar to her. The woman hadn't participated in the afterschool operations very often, but Lisa definitely remembered her face. Her eyes lit up with the light of recognition. "I remember you, now, Mrs. Mathis."

Eleanor nodded her head. "And I also remember you from this past Sunday. You came to church with my son."

Lisa hadn't realized that Eleanor was Jason's mom. Now that she'd made the connection, and since Tiffany was standing close by, Lisa figured that now was the perfect time to stick it to the bougie-acting heifer. She smiled sweetly at Mrs. Mathis and said in a slightly louder than required voice, "Oh, you're Jason's mama! Your son is such a sweetheart. Not only did he bring me to church yesterday, but he also took me out to dinner. Over at Red Sizzler — you know the nice, expensive soul food restaurant downtown? You did an excellent job on raising that boy." Lisa nodded her head. "There should be more Jason Mathises in the world. It sure 'nough would be a better place if there were."

Eleanor blushed from Lisa's compliment. Her

children were her pride and joy and it always gave her pleasure when someone acknowledged that she'd done a halfway decent job in raising them.

As for Tiffany, she'd of course heard everything. She wanted to put her fist down Lisa's throat when she heard about Jason actually taking her out on a date. *He ain't never took my black ass to Red Sizzler. In fact, he ain't never taken me out on a date to nowhere. The nicer I tried to be to him, the more he shuts me down. I hate Lisa's ass.*

Lisa glanced over at Tiffany to check on the effect of her words. She could tell from the look on the girl's face that her little comment had indeed worked the magic that she'd been hoping it was going to work. *Two points for Lisa and zero for Tiffany. Take that, trick!*

When Lisa got home that night, she figured that things had went so well in her plan to irritate Tiffany that she wanted to up the ante. She laid down on her bed on her back and stared at the ceiling. "But what can I do to get Jason to ask me out?" She whispered to the empty guest room. Then the season baseball tickets that she had to the Atlanta Braves games popped up into her mind. She liked baseball, but nobody else that she knew really did, so she hadn't even been using them. *He's a cop*, she thought to herself. *I see on TV that a lot of cops like*

*baseball. Maybe he likes it.*

Her face suddenly lit up. *Maybe he'll want to take advantage of that second ticket that I have. I'm gonna insist that we go to the games together though, of course.*

She pulled out her cellphone and scanned her contact list for his phone number. He'd given her his digits when he'd agreed to take her to church with him the past Sunday.

She smiled when she found what she was looking for and dialed his number with a quickness.

Jason had just climbed into bed for the evening when he heard his cellphone ringing. When he saw Lisa Washington's name pop up on his caller ID, he smiled. He'd been thinking about her off and on ever since Sunday. He'd even felt the urge to call her a couple of times, just to check on her and see how she was doing, but he'd pretty much chickened out at the last minute.

He'd been dreaming about Lisa every night lately, too. He suspected that he was attracted to her, but he didn't know what to think about all of that just yet.

He was thinking on her so hard, that her call actually went to his voicemail. He frowned and pressed the button, calling her right back.

"Hi, Lisa. It's me, Jason."

Lisa smiled. "Hey, Jason. I was just now leaving you a voicemail message. I know it's kinda late, so I figured you were maybe already in bed."

"Yeah, I just climbed into bed a minute or so ago.

How's things been going for you?"

"Pretty good, actually. I went to Bible study over at your church tonight. I remember that you had told me that you work late on Wednesday evenings, so I wasn't exactly expecting to see you there. But I had a really good time. And I met your mother." She grinned. "Or rather I should say I was reintroduced to your mother. I remember her from when me and my brothers and sisters used to go to Ebenezer's afterschool program… You know, for a snack and tutoring and whatnot. She's just as sweet as she was back then."

Jason smiled. "So you talked to my mom, huh? I'm sure she probably initiated that little conversation." He chuckled. "She was on the phone calling me Sunday evening after I had taken you out to dinner. She's been on my back about getting married lately — in a good type of way, of course." He laughed again. "Since I brought you to church with me, and I've never brought a female there like that before, she was wondering if you're maybe a prospective daughter-in-law for her."

"Is that right?" She let out a little laugh and didn't wait for him to answer. "If I had known that, I would've cleared the air for her. Ain't no way you would be interested in a woman like myself. I'm sure you're looking for a church girl type of sista. Somebody who has first lady type characteristics."

Jason surprised her by saying, "You know you could easily become a woman like that, don't you Lisa? You already have it in your heart to. I can see it. There's a strong woman of faith lurking right below the surface in you, girl. You have a beautiful character."

"You think so, Jason?"

Even though he knew she couldn't see him, he nodded his head and said, "I know so. I don't like telling lies. What I'm saying is the truth."

She couldn't deny it. Him saying that made her feel some type of away — a good type of way. That was one of the best compliments she'd ever received about herself — and she was a beautiful woman, so she'd received more than her fair share of compliments in her life. Mostly from men who were trying to get between her legs though. However, none of those compliments compared to the one that Jason had just given her. It felt good to know that somebody thought that she had a beautiful character.

She was really vibing from his compliment, but she decided to move on to the reason for her call. "Thanks, Jason. Now about why I was calling you in the first place... I have two season tickets to the Atlanta Braves games. In the movies and all, cops always like baseball games. But nobody around me enjoys going — I ain't been to but one game this year and the season's halfway over with. I was wondering if you wanted to take advantage of that ticket and go to a few ball games with me."

"You have Atlanta Braves season tickets, girl?"

Lisa smiled. "Yeah. It sounds like you're excited about that. Like I said, wanna go? It won't cost you a thing — correction, it's gonna cost you your time—," she giggled, "—and maybe a hot dog or two for me. But that's it."

"I love baseball. I definitely wanna take you up on that offer, Lisa. Their next game is Friday. Are we going?"

She laughed. "Yeah. That sounds like a good idea to me."

He laughed, too. "Not only will I buy your a couple of stadium hot dogs, I'll also spring for some Cracker Jacks and a soda pop. How that sound to you?"

"Sounds good, Jason."

Friday evening couldn't get there fast enough for Lisa. Yeah, she was going out with Jason because she wanted to irritate Tiffany, but she realized that she genuinely like the man. She'd enjoyed all the time that she'd spent with him — even that first day when he'd been questioning her down at the police station.

She was glad that she still had nice clothes in her closet, despite being broke and jobless. She slipped into her favorite pair of True Religion jeans. Then she slipped a cute, but casual, blouse over her head. Next, she pulled a pair of matching Jordans onto her feet. Large gold hoop earrings completed her look — a look that she knew was on point.

Her smooth brown skin was perfectly clear and flawless, so she didn't even need any makeup. Just a swipe of lip gloss and a coat of mascara on her long, natural lashes and she was done.

Staring at her reflection in her bedroom mirror in approved, she convinced herself that she wasn't trying to look good for Jason.

She smiled at herself. "I'm just doing all of this because I like looking cute."

She ignored the voice in her subconscious mind that said: *Yeah, right.*

Jason picked her up at the exact time that he said he would — six o'clock on the nose — and they headed on over to the stadium.

When they made it to their destination, Jason got Lisa's car door, just like he'd done when he'd picked her up from her mama's house twenty minutes ago. She smiled to herself. *This boy is gonna have me spoiled rotten by the time all of this is over with...with him getting my doors for me and whatnot.*

"What's so funny, Lisa?" he asked as they headed towards their seats.

"I was just thinking to myself that you're spoiling

me."

"Spoiling you? How?"

"You opening my door all the time and whatnot."

"You deserve to be spoiled, Lisa. Didn't you know that?"

"You deserve to be spoiled, too, Jason. That's why the idea of offering you that other season ticket that I had popped up in my mind."

"Well, thank you for your very generous offer, Lisa. It sure is appreciated." He paused for a moment then added, "Oh, yeah. I forgot to ask you over the phone the other day… What area of the stadium are they good for? Maybe I can spring to get us an upgrade on our seats."

She grinned again. "Dugout infield."

His eyes lit up. "Dugout infield? Are you serious, girl?"

She nodded her head. She'd known that he was gonna be pleased that they had the best seats in the stadium. At a hundred and seventy-five dollars a pop, seats in that area weren't exactly cheap.

"I could kiss you right now," he said.

The funny thing is, Lisa realized that she wouldn't have minded that. But since she knew he was kidding, she laughed and said, "You already offered to buy my snacks while we're here, I'll settle for that being thanks enough."

Lisa and Jason cheered the Braves on to a victory that night. They both left the stadium with smiles on their faces. Jason got Lisa settled into his SUV, then he came around to the driver's side of the vehicle and they began making their way out of the stadium.

She grinned over at him. "It's only a little past nine. I don't really feel like going home just yet... What about you?"

"You know what... I don't feel like going home right now either. There's a park on the other side of the stadium. We gorged ourselves on hotdogs and cheese fries in there. How about we go walk some of that off?"

Lisa had a look of doubt in her eyes when she glanced over at him. "A park? Are you for real?"

He nodded his head.

She laughed. "What I really should be saying is... Is it safe?"

"Before I became a detective, I was a regular ol' patrol officer. I was assigned to walk a beat in the district that I'm about to take you to. I assure you, the park we're getting ready to go to is safe... I wouldn't take you anywhere that isn't. And, I wouldn't let anything happen to you, Lisa."

Him saying that — that he wouldn't let anything happen to her — made her feel all warm and cuddly on the inside. *Bruh-man on a roll tonight. If this was a real date, I'd probably be about ready to give up the panties by now. And he ain't even macking or trying to sweettalk me.*

She didn't understand why she was feeling any of that, but she knew that she wanted to go take that walk with Jason.

She smiled. "I would say lead the way, but since you're the one who's doing the driving, I'll say: Get me over there already."

He laughed. "Your wish is my command, Ms. Bossy."

She shook her head in disagreement, but laughed, too. "Not Ms. Bossy, but Ms. Boss. There's a big difference, Jason Mathis."

"All right...Ms. Boss."

It turned out that Jason was right about the park. It was a hidden gem in the center of the city. A gem that was well-lit and to the most part safe — there were a couple of police officers patrolling and Lisa was fairly certain that their presence contributed to the safety factor.

They'd been strolling at a slow pace for about ten minutes when she looked over at him and said. "I've lived in Atlanta all my life. How come I'd never heard of this place?"

"It's a private park. Most people don't know that it even exists. You saw how it was hidden through all those trees and those wrought iron gates… Right?"

"Yeah." She winked her eye. "I think I wanna keep this place a secret." She giggled. "At least from most of the people I know. They'd run up in here and ruin it."

It was crazy, but knowing about that park's existence made Lisa feel a little closer to Jason. It's as if they had a secret that only the two of them knew about — a good one. In a sense, it even felt magical. And she liked that.

An hour later, she was back home, showered and lying in bed in her mother's guest room. With thoughts of the day she'd spent with Jason on her mind, she smiled. Then she did something she hadn't done in a long time. She placed her hands together and closed her eyes. Then she thanked God for the wonderful day he had given her. She even tagged on an *Amen* to the end of her little phrase of thanks.

# *C*HAPTER 6

"Man, Jason. You over there slipping, bruh. I thought you would've been finished closing out that Michael Peterson file an hour ago."

Sitting behind his desk downtown at the police station on Monday morning, Jason glanced over at his coworker, Detective Tony Roberts. He frowned. "I had a lot of stuff on my mind this morning, Tony...a whole of stuff."

Tony chuckled. "Based on the way you were smiling to yourself as you worked on that file, I know that the whole lot of stuff you just said you have on your mind has to do with a woman. What's her name, man?"

Jason saw no reason to deny it. "Her name's Lisa."

"Well, this Lisa certainly has you caught up, bruh. I know a few Lisa's. Your Lisa, is she one of the ones that I might know about? Like Lisa from downstairs in accounting...the one with the big rack and even bigger tha-dunk-a-dunk."

Jason shook his head. "Man, why you always describing women by their physical assets?"

Tony grinned. "Because that's what I notice about a woman the most. But back on the subject… Do you think I know her?"

"Not really. You remember that casino case from a couple of weeks, don't you?"

"Yep. That was one of our biggest busts of the year so far. What does that have to do with anything though?"

"You remember the girl I investigated, right? Or rather the one I questioned. She's the one that you were originally supposed to go in and interrogate, but because you got called upstairs to handle that Russian mafia case at the last minute, I ended up having to question her for you."

Tony turned his lips up in a smile and a mischievous glint came into his eyes. "How could I not forget? Homegirl was fine. A real dime piece. I was kinda disappointed when upstairs reassigned me."

Jason didn't appreciate the look of lust that had come into his coworker's eyes when he'd mentioned Lisa. In fact, Jason felt like bringing the conversation to a close. However, a look of understanding came onto Tony's face and he said, "That girl's the one who's got you over there trippin'… Ain't she, man? She's the one."

Jason frowned. Not because he was feeling bad about how he felt about Lisa, but because he didn't like the way

Tony was lusting after her.

Tony chuckled. "My bad, J. I didn't know you were feeling her like that. Tell you what I'll do… I'll go ahead and erase all the inappropriate thoughts I was having about what I'd do to her if she were my woman — you know, the thoughts I was having on that evening that y'all brought her in." He closed his eyes real hard and massaged his temples, pretending that he was erasing something from the sides of his head. He chuckled. Then he opened his eyes and looked directly at Jason. "There you go, man. It's all erased. Now tell me what's going on between the two of you. I'm assuming you've had some type of contact with her since that night you let her walk up out here."

Jason understood that Tony knew that he'd let Lisa walk. But it was all good though, because Tony and Jason had been working together for five years. They knew that judgement calls were occasionally part of the policing game. Neither of the men did things like that often — let someone go free when they shouldn't have — but it happened from time to time. Not for anything major of course. Just minor offenses where the person really shouldn't have been charged anyway. And both of the men understood that it was comparable to a patrol officer giving a person a speeding warning when they had the option to dole out a ticket instead, because the person had indeed been driving above the posted speed limit.

"Tell me about her, Jason."

Jason made up his mind that he was going to go ahead and open up about it. "She's nothing like you would've imagined, Tony. She's a real sweet girl with a good heart."

He nodded his head and continued speaking. "I told you that somebody had been dropping a five-hundred dollar donation off every month over at Ebenezer Christian Center. Turns out it was my Lisa." He smiled and corrected himself. "I mean it was Lisa… It was the girl that I was telling you about. I caught her leaving the donation the same morning that I was dropping off mine. And there's other good things about her, too. From first glance, she might come off seeming ghetto-fabulous or something. But she's not like that at all. She's smart and resourceful. She's trying to make herself into an even better person. She's trying to change her life."

"Seems like she's really impressed you, bruh."

"She has, Tony. She most definitely has."

"So… You told her how you're feeling about her yet?"

"Naw… Not yet. Tell you the truth, man. I just figured out how I was feeling about her my ownself. I realized that I liked her when I took her to church two Sundays ago, but I somehow convinced myself that it was just some type of passing attraction." He shook his head. "When I couldn't get her outta my mind for the past few days, I started thinking that it might be something that's a little more than just a fly-by-night type of thing." His eyes met Tony's "Know what I mean?"

Tony chuckled. "I know what you mean all right. Big Bad Jason Mathis finally got himself bitten by the lovebug. You falling in love, man."

Jason thought about what Tony had said all day that day. At six o'clock that evening, he finally clocked out from work and left to go home. Him and Lisa had made plans to catch the next Braves home game in ten days. He figured that chances were high that he wouldn't be seeing her until then. *I guess I'm gonna have ten days to sort out how I feel about her. I know that I'm catching feelings for her, but is it possible that I really am falling in love? Is Tony right?*

He shook his head. Then, instead of going home, he took the exit that would take him to his parents' house. He had a tight relationship with his dad. He wanted to see what his father had to say about all of this.

"Hey there, son. I figured that I wouldn't be seeing you until Sunday in church. What brings you by here to visit your ol' pops today. What's going on?"

Jason's father, Ervin, was at the back of his house hand washing his Cadillac XTS. The car was his baby and he treated it with kid gloves.

"Hey, dad. I was hoping you could take a break and shoot the breeze with me for a minute or two."

Ervin stopped what he was doing. He tilted his head to the side and studied his son for a few seconds. "This sounds serious."

"It is kind of serious — well, at least to me it is. Really, I just need your advice on something. I don't know a man in Atlanta who gives better advice than you."

Ervin went back to moving the cleaning sponge in slow, wide circles. Then he said, "Get the hose and wash the soap off my caddie. Then meet me inside in the study. We can talk."

Ten minutes later, Ervin listened patiently as his oldest son shared details about the situation involving a young woman he was apparently interested in. When it sounded like Jason had finished speaking his piece, Ervin nodded his head in understanding and said, "So I guess what you're asking me is do I think you're falling in love with this young lady, or if it's something else...like infatuation. Because two short weeks ain't exactly a lot of time to be falling in love with nobody."

Jason nodded his head. He had known his father would understand. "Yeah, dad." He pinched his chin between his thumb and his forefinger a few time. "That's what I was wondering."

"Right. Now I can't say for sure whether or not you're falling for this girl, but one thing I know is that it's very possible." Ervin chuckled. "Truth be told, I fell head over heels for your mama after only ten days of knowing her. We Mathis men might just have it like that. We might just know what we want almost from the second we first lay eyes on it. Know what I mean?"

Jason nodded his head again, acknowledging that he'd understood what his father had just told him.

A serious expression suddenly took over Ervin's facial features. "You're a man of faith, son. If this girl is the one for you, God'll let you know it in your spirit. You'll feel it. You'll find yourself going through your day, and all you're gonna be able to think about is this girl. Then you'll notice that her safety and well-being is the number one goal in your life — outside of your commitment to God, of course. Next you'll notice that you'd gladly lay down your own life for this woman. When you feel all three of those things, you'll know for sure that you're in love…that she's the one who's captured your heart."

Ervin smiled again. "As for right now, I recommend that the two of you start seriously dating." He chuckled. "That's a good first step right there."

"Dating?"

"Yeah. You know, call her on the phone and invite her out to dinner and maybe a movie. Get your macking game on, son." He smiled. "What? You young folks don't do that no more?"

Jason chuckled, too. "I know how to ask her out on a

date, dad." Then he gave his father a man hug of appreciation. "Thanks for everything."

Jason really appreciated his father's advice. He hoped that when he someday had a son, his kid would be comfortable coming to him about any and everything — just like Jason was comfortable with going to his father.

As he hit the interstate and made his way home, he began imagining what his and Lisa's kids would look like if they ever got together. He smiled to himself. *We're not at that stage yet. I think I better go ahead and take my father's advice and make some moves towards us seriously dating.*

Now that he had formulated a game plan for himself, he didn't feel like waiting. As soon as he made it home, he pulled out his cellphone and dialed Lisa's number.

*Across Town*:

Sitting in a booth at Taco Bell having a quick cheap meal with Carmen and Janelle, Lisa laughed at a joke that Carmen had just told them. Then, when her phone started ringing she said, "Wait a minute, ladies. Jason's calling me. I'm gonna have to put you two heifers on hold."

Janelle chuckled. "We were her girls till ol' boy rang her number. Now we just heifers." She turned to Carmen and asked, "What you think about that, Carmen? She just put bros before hoes. Is that messed up or what?"

As Lisa picked up her phone, Carmen shook her head at Janelle. Then she whispered, "We'll forgive her this time, Janelle. She *did* drive both of us over here and she footed the bill for our food. She ain't even ask for any gas to put in her tank. And you know that Benz be drinking gasoline like it ain't nobody's business." Carmen held her finger up to her lips in a shushing motion. "So let's keep the noise level down. She 'bout to get on the phone."

Since Lisa didn't trust her two friends to be quiet as she took her phone call, she stood up and excused herself. She had decided to talk to Jason just outside of the front door of the restaurant.

"Hi, Jason. What's up?" she asked as she walked towards the restaurant door.

"I must be special," he said into his phone and chuckled. "You put my name into your caller ID. That's how you knew it was me calling."

"I hope my name's beside my number in your phone, too. You and I can't help but be friends. We're the only black Atlanta Braves fans on this side of town. We gotta stick together."

He laughed again. "You might just have a point with that right there."

"Yeah, I know right. Now what's up? To what do I owe the pleasure of hearing that deep baritone voice of yours this evening?"

He jumped right into it. "I was hoping I could get you interested in going out to dinner with me — maybe this weekend. You giving me that season pass to the Braves game deserves some type of payback. Something besides me buying you hot dogs and cracker jacks. What do you say, Lisa? You gonna let me take you out this Friday or Saturday?"

To Lisa, it felt like he was asking her out on a real date. But she was sure that he wasn't doing that. *Now that I'm single, I guess I'm getting thirsty. I guess I'm getting all needy for some attention. But I'm not that church girl that Jason would want to go out with. He's just being nice. I'm sure he's not asking me out on a real date.*

She had definitely thought all of that. However, she intended on taking him up on his offer because that meant she'd have some more fuel to agitate Tiffany with. *Nothing wrong with her assuming we're going out together for real.*

Then she suddenly had a great idea. She knew that Tiffany's father owned a restaurant in town — it was called Greenbow Soul Food Station. She smiled into her phone. "I love the food at Greenbow Soul Food Station. You think we can hit them up?"

"Sure, Lisa. Friday or Saturday?"

*The sooner, the better*, she thought to herself. "Friday sounds good to me."

They disconnected their call a minute or so later, and

Lisa made her way back to the booth that she, Carmen, and Janelle were sharing.

"Oh, Lord," Carmen said as soon as she saw the look on Lisa's face. "What's up with that crazy-looking little smile of yours, boo?"

"Jason just asked me out on another date. We're hitting up Greenbow Soul Food Station on Friday night."

Carmen drew her eyebrows together in a worried frown. "Ain't that the restaurant that Tiffany's father owns?"

Lisa folded herself into her seat at their booth. "It sure is. And I hope Tiffany is helping out there Friday night. That would be perfect." She shrugged her shoulders. "Either way, if she's not there, I'm sure one of her other family members is gonna tell her that Jason was up in the joint with me. It's gonna be win-win all the way around — except for Tiffany of course. That trick ain't winning nothing—," Lisa frowned., "—except some disappointment."

"Don't you think you're taking this a little bit too far, Lisa?" Carmen asked.

Lisa rolled her eyes. "Naw, boo... I actually don't. She shoulda been thinking that way back in high school when her and Angela kept picking on me because my clothes were out of season, old, and whack." The hurt from those days was still in Lisa's heart. "I probably would've never gotten with Big Ron if I hadn't been feeling the pressure to have nicer things in life. Tiffany was foul... And she still is."

After Lisa had said that, Carmen didn't say another word that day on that topic She realized that Lisa was carrying a load of pain in her heart from how Tiffany had treated her. Back in high school, Lisa had been the type of person who tried to stay out of confrontations and fights. She'd gone a long time without laying a hand on Tiffany — despite all the mess Tiffany had liked to talk, simply because Lisa had wanted to stay outta trouble. *Lord,* Carmen said to herself. *Please heal my girl's heart.*

Lisa glanced over at Janelle. "What do you think, Janelle? Do you think what I'm doing is crazy?"

Janelle shook her head. "Naw. I don't think what you doing is crazy at all. If you ask me — and you did — people getting away with shit ain't right. I didn't go to highschool with y'all, but everything y'all told me about this Tiffany chick points to her being a real piece of work. Bout like my husband that I ended up gunning down — just to keep him from kicking my ass."

*But everything like that comes with a price,* Carmen thought to herself. Carmen had shot her boyfriend in self defense and she'd served seven hard years for her efforts — even though he hadn't died. She frowned. "Just remember, ladies... *Vengeance is mine saith the Lord.* That comes straight from the Bible and it means that God will fight our battles. Turn your life over to the Lord, Lisa—," she looked over at Janelle, "—and you, too, Janelle. God will fight y'all battles for you." She smiled.

"Now since I don't feel like preaching up in here, let's change the subject."

Both Carmen and Janelle were all for that.

*Later on that Night:*

Lisa pulled her car up to her mother's house and parked it along the curb. She'd just finished dropping Carmen and Janelle off at the halfway house that they both lived in. Now she was sitting alone in her Benz reflecting on everything that had gone down earlier that evening. She stayed out there a good ten minutes thinking on it, then when she went into the house, she still had it on her mind.

She made quick work of taking her shower and getting into bed. It was at that moment that she suddenly had an idea. *I'm gonna go on Facebook and see if I can send some of Tiffany's friends some friend requests. Then I'm gonna post snapshots of me and Jason from our dates online. I already got pics of us at the ball stadium. I'mma get even more of us when we go out to dinner Friday night.* She smiled to herself. *I'm sure Tiffany is gonna end up seeing the pics. That should really piss her off.*

It was almost a half hour later — and she was half the way asleep — when Lisa realized that she hadn't said her now ritualist single-line prayer for the night. She placed her palms together in front of her face in the traditional prayer stance. Then she thanked God for keeping her safe that day and in a solemn voice she said *Amen.*

# CHAPTER 7

Lisa thought it was weird, but when Wednesday evening rolled around, she was feeling the urge to go to Bible study again. She didn't even own a Bible, so she was glad that the church would be providing her one to use while she was there. She was even more surprised that she'd now gotten into the habit of saying a prayer before she would go to bed at night. Yeah, it was only one–line long, but it was a prayer all the same. And she now found herself talking to God every now and then throughout her day.

When Friday evening arrived, she made sure that her look was more than on point for her little date with Jason at Tiffany's father's restaurant. All of her clothes were top-notch designer selections and she'd beat her face to perfection.

She smiled at her reflection in her bedroom mirror. "Shoot, I look like I belong on the cover of Essence

Magazine or something. If I must say so myself, I'm looking mighty good this evening...downright fly. Them pictures that I'm about to put on Facebook of me and Jason from this evening are gonna be slamming."

Her heart did a little funny pitter-patter in her chest from thinking about Jason. She smiled. *He's a good man... A really good man. I like him. He's gonna make one of them church girls down at Ebenezer a damn good husband.*

She frowned when she had that last thought. Then she sighed and shook her head. For some reason, she didn't like imagining Jason married and off the market. *I better get on outside on the front porch so I can wait on him. He'll be here in a minute.*

She preferred meeting Jason outside because she didn't feel like hearing any lip from her mama about him. She already knew that Diane Washington was gonna assume that her oldest daughter was dating again. *Not only is she gonna assume that, but she's also gonna start harping on about how I finally snagged a good man this time. Then I'm gonna have to explain to her that Jason ain't feeling me like that. I don't even wanna go there.*

Unfortunately for Lisa, she walked out of her bedroom door at least a half minute too late. By the time she'd made it to the living room, her mama was smiling up into Jason's face.

Diane turned around and beamed at her daughter. "Lisa, your date is here and I've only been talking to him a few seconds and I can tell that I like this one. He ain't nothing like that no good fool, Big Ron." Then she looked Jason in the face. "You said your name was Jason, didn't you?"

Jason grinned. "Yes, ma'am."

To Lisa, her mama's first statement had been bad. But she felt like crawling under a bus when her mom said, "Y'all look so cute...so cute that I wanna snap myself a picture of the two of you before you leave." She held out her hand, palm facing forward and added, "Wait right there. I'mma go get my cellphone."

As soon as Diane ran out the room, Lisa looked over at Jason with the heat of a blush in her cheeks. She shook her head. "Jason, I'm so sorry about my mama."

He smiled. "It's okay, Lisa. All mamas who love their kids are like that. My mom would probably be doing the same thing in this situation." He winked his eye. "I have to admit though, it's comforting to know that she thinks I'm an improvement on Big Ron. I would've been embarrassed if she thought I had downgraded you."

She couldn't help but smile herself from the little joke that Jason had just made. She looked him in the eye and said, "If we move real quick, we might actually be able to slip out of here before she gets back. My mama can't ever remember where she put her cellphone. It always takes her at least a minute to find it once she gets up in the house real good."

Jason chuckled. "Naw, we're not giving her the slip

like that. She might not let me take you out again if that's the case. Then I'd be sad."

*He's making this sound like a real date.* She got excited at that prospect. Then she shut down her thinking along that little path. *He ain't checking for you, fool*, she admonished herself.

She pointed at him. "Well, at least you look good."

His eyes met hers. He smiled. "And you do, too. You're a very beautiful woman, Lisa. You'd make an old, dusty burlap sack look nice."

Using one of her girl Carmen's favorite phrases, Lisa thought to herself: *Lawd have mercy*. She felt like fanning herself on account of him making that last little statement.

At that point, Lisa was more than happy that her mother had found her cellphone and had stepped back into the living room. She hadn't known what to say in response to Jason's compliment. Somehow, a simple thank you hadn't seemed like it would suffice.

They allowed her mother to take her pictures — which Lisa now figured was a good thing because she had every intention of posting them on Facebook so that Tiffany would end up seeing them. Then the couple got on their way.

Despite her knowing that they weren't on a real date,

Lisa was feeling like a Disney Princess. Jason had just gotten her door for her — like he'd been doing ever since they'd first met — and now he'd surprised her by presenting her with a single white rose. Nobody had ever given her flowers before. Nobody. Not ever. That made her feel really special.

He backed his SUV out of the driveway and smiled over at Lisa. "Most guys like to give out red or pink roses to women. I wanted to give you a white one, Lisa."

"Why is that? Why did you want to give me a white one instead of any other color?"

He grinned again. "Because white represents purity and you have this pureness about yourself. I know your life circumstances might be trying to dull and destroy that, but it's still there. I can see it shining. It's radiating from you like the brightest evening star."

Yeah, a look of doubt instantly made its way into her soft brown eyes. "Me? You're talking about me? As in Lisa Denise Washington?"

He surprised her by reaching across the center console and taking her hand into his. Then he gave it a tiny squeeze. "Yeah, girl. I'm talking about you. It's there. You're a good person at heart, Lisa. I told you that you were beautiful back at your mama's house. But your beauty is more than just a physical thing. It's even more than skin deep. You have a beautiful heart, girl."

That was a first, too. In other words, nobody had ever said anything like that to her. And she could tell that

Jason meant every single word that he'd said...he wasn't trying to run no game on her. He was dead serious, and that made her feel good on the inside. It made her feel good that someone had noticed her heart. She had a natural tendency to be decent by people — that's why she'd been making anonymous donations to the afterschool program at Ebenezer Christian Center for years. And that's why she hadn't whooped Tiffany's butt well before their senior year.

She blushed. Then she finally smiled. "Thank you, Jason. And you have a beautiful heart, too."

Her emotions were starting to go a little haywire, so she decided that she needed to bring some lightness to their conversation. Accordingly, she said, "I guess we have two reasons why we're friends now: We're both Braves fans and we both have decent hearts." She laughed. "Now back to the Braves fan thing. I hope you know you taking me out to dinner tonight doesn't nullify you buying me hot dogs and cracker jacks next week?"

He released Lisa's left hand from his and placed his hand back on the steering wheel. He chuckled. "Yeah. I think I understand that."

Fifteen minutes later, Jason was pulling Lisa's chair out for her at Greensbow Soul Food Station. From the moment they'd set foot inside of the restaurant, Lisa had been scanning the room for Tiffany. Tiffany wasn't there, but her bestie, Angela, was. Lisa noticed her a few seconds after Jason had pushed her chair up to the table, and of course Angela was throwing Lisa a nasty look. Lisa hadn't been expecting anything less from the girl.

Since she knew how petty both Angela and Tiffany were, Lisa made up in her mind that she was going to order the exact same thing that Jason got that evening. *That heifer might wanna spit in my food or something. If Jason and I have the same meal, that'll cut down on her wanting to pull that little stunt. She gonna be thinking that there's a possibility that Jason will get the messed up plate, since they're both gonna look the same.*

Lisa didn't relish the idea of eating food that somebody had spit in. But she couldn't help but think that the look she'd seen on Angela's face a few seconds ago would make it worth it. *Angela telling Tiffany what she witnessed would definitely make it more than worth it*, Lisa thought to herself as she frowned.

She normally would've smiled from having a thought like that. But now that Jason had made his comment about her having a good heart, she was starting to rethink some things. Then she began thinking back over the Bible study session that she'd participated in earlier that week. It had focused on situations where Christians should and shouldn't turn the other cheek. Something within her was starting to tell her that maybe she should be turning the other cheek on how Tiffany had treated her.

"You okay, Lisa?" Jason asked.

She pushed aside the thoughts she'd been having.

She gave him a smile. "Yeah. I'm fine. What are you having tonight?"

"I think I'll go with the oxtails. With a side of mac & cheese, along with some cabbage. And of course cornbread." He smiled. "It just wouldn't be a real soul food meal without cornbread."

She nodded her head. "Yeah. I feel ya, Jason. I'm getting all of that, too."

Angela had been working as a junior executive in downtown Atlanta. But she'd been laid off from her job eight months ago. Now she was back to waiting tables as her full-time gig. The second she laid eyes on Lisa and Jason in that restaurant, she knew she had to tell her girl, Tiffany, about it. She didn't even want to wait.

Angela pulled out her cell phone and discreetly snapped a real quick pic. In the photo that she'd taken, Jason was covering Lisa's hand with his own, and the two were looking into each other's faces and laughing about something. *Tiffany's gonna need a picture to really understand this shit.*

*An Hour Later*:

Lisa looked across Jason's SUV at him and smiled. "Why do I end up stuffed like a sausage whenever you take me out anywhere, Jason Mathis? Huh?"

He winked his eye. "I'm just trying to make sure that my date for the evening is well taken care of. You might not wanna go out with me again if I don't." He laughed. "If it'll make you feel any better, you're not the only one who's feeling stuffed. Wanna go take a walk? You know, like we did the last time?"

"You know what, Jason? I think I'm actually up for that. But that park you took me to the last time is way on the other side of town."

"There's another one that I know you'll enjoy. It's on this side of town… On the outskirts. It'll only take ten minutes to get there. Are you game?"

"Yep." She laughed. "I'mma have to make you my unofficial park guide or something. I'm interested to see where you're taking me to tonight."

Lisa had had other things to do with her time over the past years — things other than hanging out in parks, even occasionally. When Jason rolled up to their destination, she realized that she'd been missing out

"It's so pretty out here, Jason.."

He opened the passenger-side door and helped her out of the SUV. He wanted to tell her that the view out there in the park didn't compare to how pretty she looked to him, but he figured that would've been laying it on too thick. He'd already complimented her earlier in the evening when he'd given her the rose. He didn't want to scare her off.

They started on a slow stroll down a wide paved

footpath. There was a handful of other couples out there that evening enjoying the ambiance of their mutual surroundings. When they passed a second couple, Jason placed his arm around Lisa's shoulders and pulled her a little closer towards the left side of the path, making room for the other couple to pass them comfortably.

Lisa understood the reason why he'd done what he'd done. But that didn't stop a tremor of awareness from passing through her body from his touch. *What in the world was that?* That's what she'd asked herself. She was confused now. She didn't exactly understand her reaction.

Jason led them over to a park bench and they took a seat. She was suddenly nervous for some reason. She was normally a very talkative type of person, but she didn't have too much to say right now.

"This is one of my favorite parks, Lisa. My mother and father used to bring me and my brothers out here when we were little." He let out a chuckle. "But always in the daytime, though. It wasn't until I was in my early twenties that I learned about how great a place this park was in the evenings."

She suddenly felt what she knew was a stab of jealousy. "You used to bring your dates out here… Right?"

He shook his head. "Nope. Not actually." He smiled. "I'm a jogger. I like coming out here to run. In the summertime, the evenings are cooler...about like right now."

After saying that, he took off his blazer and placed it around Lisa's shoulders. It was August in Atlanta — technically summer. They'd been experiencing a cool snap for some reason for the past couple of days, and the highs during the day had only been in the 70s. Right now, Lisa guessed that the temperature was maybe about sixty-five or so. So yeah, it was a slight bit on the cool side out there that night.

She appreciated Jason's gesture, and she'd just experienced another first. She'd never had a man to take the coat off his own back and place it on hers, just because it was a tiny bit nippy outside. She was starting to feel like she was in one of those romantic movies and she was the star. That she was the love interest that the hero was yearning for. That she was the one who was about to get a happily-ever-after.

She brought her thinking back down to Earth. *I ain't no Cinderella, and this definitely ain't no fairy tale. Get real, Lisa.*

He pointed up at the stars. "I like coming out here to stare at the stars sometimes, too. When I was a kid, I used to find the brightest star in the sky, and make a wish on it." He wrapped his hand around her wrist and raised her arm up. "Point out your finger," he instructed.

She didn't know what he was up to, but she did as he told her. He smiled. "That's the brightest star. That one right there. It's called Sirius. Go ahead and close your eyes and make a wish on it."

Wishing on stars. To Lisa, that indeed was something straight from a fairy tale. She looked over at Jason and returned his smile with one of her own. "Are you serious?"

He nodded his head. "Yeah. Nothing wrong with making wishes, Lisa. They're like prayers. It's like you're speaking from your soul and asking God to do something for you. When I was little, I used to imagine that that star was a special extra bright globe in Heaven that God collected people's prayers out of. I used to imagine that he'd reach his hand right into it, pull out a person's prayer, and read it. You can do the same if you want to." He chuckled.

It sounded a little corny, but Lisa felt the urge to do it anyway. She closed her eyes tight and said a prayer to herself. She prayed that God would come into her life.

When she opened her eyes, he was smiling at her. "All done?"

She grinned, too. "Yeah."

Jason hoped and prayed that Lisa got whatever thing she'd just asked for. He wanted to see her happy.

She surprised him by saying, "Thanks for praying that my prayer would come true."

"How'd you know that's what I was praying for?" he asked.

She winked her eye. "I'm not the only one sitting on this here bench who has a good heart, Jason Mathis. No what I mean?"

"I think so."

She leaned back into the wrought iron backing of her seat. "You're lucky to have had parents who brought you out to places like this when you were a kid. I grew up in the projects. They had a park out there — a playground really, with a few park benches under the trees." She smiled as somewhat fond memories of those days came back to her. "That was about as far as my mama went when it came down to taking us to the park...or anywhere really. We didn't have a car while I was growing up. If we went somewhere, we either had to walk or take the bus. There were six of us kids. Needless to say, taking the bus all around town could've ended up being expensive."

"What about your dad? Was he ever in the picture?"

"To the most part, my mom is a good woman. But she wasn't always saved like she is now. I don't know my father, Jason. It was some guy that my mama met while she was out clubbing one night. They dated for about a week and I was conceived. Then he skipped town. My mama never saw him or heard from him again. She even thinks he gave her a fictitious name."

He took her hand into his and gave it a squeeze of support. "I'm sorry to hear that, Lisa."

She wasn't gonna try to front. Growing up not knowing who her dad was had been a hurtful thing. It still hurted sometimes. She really didn't like opening up like that to anybody. But there was something about Jason, and there was something about the evening that they were sharing that made her feel comfortable enough to speak her piece and spill her guts.

"What about you, Jason? What was your childhood like?"

She knew the answer to her question, even before she'd asked it. *He had a charmed childhood, I'm sure of it. About like the freaking Cosby Kids... Or the Brady Bunch.*

She was surprised to see a shadow settle on his face — a look of sadness. "My childhood was decent. But it wasn't without its problems. I had a little sister — she was a year and a half younger than me. From the time I was five until I was ten, I had to watch her suffer from cancer. Leukemia. She passed away when she was only nine. I was angry at God for years because of her passing. I didn't understand how a loving and just God could let my sister suffer like that. I went through a lot of trials and tribulations. It wasn't until I turned twenty-three, almost a decade ago, that I decided to let God back into my life. There's an old gospel song called We'll Understand It Better By and By. I began to take solace in that song, to take comfort in it. We don't always understand the reason why God does things — because after all, like the Bible says in Isaiah 55 and 8: *God's thoughts are not our thoughts and his ways are not our ways*. But one thing for sure, Lisa, when I meet God, I'll also see my sister again. And I'll understand everything at that time. I have faith in that. I know it."

Lisa's family had been blessed to the most part. She had two younger brothers and one of them was only a year younger than her. They had grown up in an area that had been rife with poverty and gang violence. She hadn't lost any of her siblings. She couldn't even imagine what she would've done and how she would've felt if she had.

Her heart went out to Jason for his loss. Now it was her turn to take his hand into hers and give it a squeeze of encouragement...a squeeze of support. "I'm so sorry, Jason."

He nodded his head. "Thank you, Lisa. I know you really mean it. That means a lot to me."

Baring their souls to each other like they'd just done seemed to have elevated their friendship to another level. Jason suddenly turned to Lisa and smiled. "You ready to go home now, kindhearted Lisa?"

"Yeah. I guess so."

When he pulled his SUV into the driveway at Lisa's mother's house, everything within Jason wanted to give Lisa a kiss goodnight. But he knew their relationship wasn't at that point yet.

He parked his vehicle and reached his hand under his seat. He glanced over at her and smiled. "I have another gift for you. It's a Bible. The NIV version, which is a whole lot easier to read and understand then the King James one. I had it personalized for you — your name is inscribed inside the front cover. I hope you enjoy it."

She took her gift from him. Then she said, "I feel guilty now, Jason. You've given me two gifts tonight and I haven't given you anything."

"I beg to differ, Lisa. You gave me plenty. Your attention and your time. Those two things right there are priceless and I thank you for them."

With that being said, he hopped out of his SUV and got the passenger-side door for her. Then he walked her to the front door of her mother's house. He smiled, then using his thumb and forefinger, he tilted up her chin and looked her in the eye. "Enjoy your Bible, Lisa. I'll see you later… Okay?"

"Okay."

Lisa stepped through the front door and closed it behind herself. Then she heard a rustling sound in the living room by the windows. Next, she noticed her mother guiltily moving away from the curtains.

"Mama! Were you peeking at me and Jason out there on that front porch?"

Diane was guilty as sin, but she shook her head and said, "What are you talking about, Lisa?"

Lisa laughed. "You couldn't be a criminal, mama. The minute the police ask you if you committed the crime, your face is gonna give you away."

Diane pretended that Lisa hadn't said a word. "How was the date? I hope you say it was good, 'cause that boy is a keeper."

"I'm sorry to bust your bubble — I know how much you want me with a saved and sanctified church boy — but we weren't on a real date. He was just being nice."

Diane humphed. Then she folded her arms over her chest. "Sure looked like a date to me." She began walking out of the living room, leaving Lisa behind her. Then she smiled to herself. She had noticed the brand-new-looking Bible in her daughter's hand. She liked seeing that. She forced a stern tone to her voice. "Don't mess things up with him, little girl. Good men are hard to come by...you hear?"

Lisa had heard all right. Her mother's words made her grimace. She still didn't think that Jason was ever gonna be interested in her like that. She shook her head. *My mama and her wishful thinking is something else.*

*Two Hours Later*:

Lisa finally closed the Bible that Jason had given her. She hadn't intended on reading it that night. But after she'd showered and gotten in bed, it seemed as if the thing had been calling her name. So she'd turn on the bedside lamp and cracked it open.

She hadn't known where to start. With most books, you start reading from the very beginning. But for some reason, Lisa hadn't felt the urge to start there. She'd opened her Bible somewhere in the middle and started reading from the top of the first page she saw. The very first verses she read were John 3:16-17, which said: *For God loved the world so much that he gave his only son, so that everyone who believes in him may not die but have eternal life. For God did not send his son into the world to be its judge, but to be its savior.*

She kept reading those two verses over and over again, and then she thumbed through the Bible, greedily reading more and more. Before she knew it, an hour had passed by and she had a smile on her face. Then she had tears in her eyes. She knew that God was real. She was feeling his presence all around her in her mama's guest room that night.

"You exist God! You exist! You're real! You! Are! REAL!" With tears pouring from her eyes and running down her cheeks, she began shouting those phrases over and over again, she couldn't help herself.

When Diane heard shouting in her house, she ran to the guest room to see what all the commotion was about. When she witnessed her oldest daughter crying out to God in happiness and submission, tears sprang into her own eyes. Her prayers had been answered. She knew right then and there that God himself had touched her child.

# CHAPTER 8

Lisa woke up the following morning with a renewed interest in life. It felt good knowing that God was indeed real. She'd had a certain jealousy in her heart when she'd heard her mama and Carmen and other people talking about feeling God — especially since she'd never felt him before.

Now that she'd experienced his touch for herself, she felt as if she could do anything. She felt as if she could *be* anything. "I am a conqueror," she whispered under her breath.

She got out of bed and grabbed her cellphone. The first thing she noticed was that she had Facebook notifications. She frowned at that. She'd been posting pictures of her and Jason doing stuff together for the past few days — all with the intention of aggravating and paying back Tiffany Scott.

Now that she'd felt God and she'd been studying her Bible a little, her self-accusing spirit was starting to kick in. She shook her head at the photos — photos she was pretty much sure Tiffany had already seen. "This ain't right, God. I can see now that this isn't how you want me acting... How you want me going about things."

A conversation that she'd had with Carmen recently popped up into her mind. Carmen had told her that God would fight battles for his followers. *I'm gonna have to let God give me justice and vengeance on this. This fight's not mine, it's the Lord's.*

She proceeded to delete the photos off of Facebook with a quickness, but she kept copies of them on her phone itself. She flopped down on the bed and studied her favorite snapshot of her and Jason together. It was one that they'd gotten the concession stand attendant to snap for them while they'd been at the Braves game.

She slowly traced her index finger along the strong profile of Jason's handsome face. Then it came to her. *I'm falling in love with him.* She frowned because she didn't welcome that.

For all of her adult life, Lisa had considered herself to be a real boss chick. In her eyes, real boss chicks didn't fall in love. They used their skills and talents — or their beauty and sex appeal — to get what they wanted out of life. That's why she had stayed with Big Ron for so long. She hadn't loved him, she'd just been using him for her own personal financial gain.

Her conscious mind then told her: *Jason would never be interested in you anyway because he wants a church girl.* It was at that point that she realized that she was probably on the path to evolving into a church girl. Now that she knew that God was real, becoming a regular churchgoer seemed like a logical next step for her to take.

She sighed to herself. Everything was so confusing to her right now. "All I probably need to be doing is focusing on keeping and growing my relationship with God. That makes the most sense to me."

*Across Town at Tiffany's House:*

Still half the way asleep, Tiffany reached her arm out toward her nightstand and snatched her ringing cellphone. *Whoever is calling me best to be calling me for a good reason. It's still morning and everybody knows I like sleeping in on Saturday mornings. I don't even have to silence my ringer, cause everybody knows not to bother me.*

She didn't even check her phone to see who was calling. As soon as she picked it up, in an irritated voice, she barked, "What do you want?"

"Good morning to you, too, Tiff."

"This had better be good, Angie... As in somebody done keeled over and died good. It ain't even nine o'clock in the morning yet."

"Don't be trying to get all mad at me. I tried to call

you last night, but you wouldn't pick up your phone."

Tiffany didn't feel like going there. "What do you want?"

"I guess you didn't see the picture I sent you yesterday."

"I told you I was gonna let Jermaine hit it last night. We were at the club partying together, and then we were getting our freak on at his place. I didn't have no time for checking no cellphone... You know that boy be laying the pipe real good. He keeps me up all night."

"Well, check it now."

Tiffany scrolled over to her text messages. The second she saw the photo of Lisa and Jason, she got hot. "What the hell?"

Angela nodded her head. "I figured that's what you'd be thinking. Lisa and Jason were all up in Greenbow last night. Laughing and giggling all in each other's faces and whatnot. You should've seen 'em, girl."

Tiffany refused to ignore her sexual needs, so she didn't have a problem with accepting a booty call from her very married coworker, Jermaine. But she still had her heart and her mind set on getting with Jason. She wanted to be Mrs. Jason Mathis.

Tiffany shook her head. "I'm sure he probably just ran into her there at the restaurant and they decided to share a table — about like what happened that morning when I saw them together at Starbucks. I know I told you that after that heifer left out the mall, I asked Jason why

116

he was sitting with her having coffee. And he told me her table had been the only one available, so he'd asked her if he could sit down… He ain't even friends with her ass."

"That might've been what happened at Starbucks, but that ain't what happened last night, boo. He walked her through the front door of Greenbow. And while we're at it, let's not forget that he brought her with him to church the other Sunday. Then I overheard her telling somebody up in Bible study that he took her to dinner after church that day. That trick is trying to steal your man, girl."

"A decent, hard-working nigga like Jason ain't gonna won't a chicken-head like Lisa. Ain't no way."

"Look, I was there last night, boo. It sure did look like he wanted her to me. I know what I saw. What you gonna do about it, Tiffany?"

Tiffany didn't know what she was gonna do. But she knew that she was going to do something. She wrapped up her phone call with Angela. She wanted to lie down and get some more sleep, but she was too tee'd off by that picture to do that.

She slid out of bed and snatched the bedcovers off of it. She threw them on the floor in anger. Then she decided to go ahead and get dressed so that she could go put in her four-hour stint at the carnival that her church was hosting.

She hadn't really wanted to help out, but that carnival was Jason's mother's pet project — every year, it raised good money for her afterschool program for kids. Tiffany had volunteered so that she could impress the woman. She really did intend on getting with Jason...as in marrying him. She figured that she might as well get in good with his mama.

*An Hour Later:*

"Hey Lisa... Guess who?"

"I don't have to guess who. I know it's you, Jason Mathis. I have your name in my caller ID... Remember?" She giggled.

"Yeah, that's right. You sound really upbeat and chipper this morning — not to say that you don't sound that way most of the time I'm talking to you — but I think you know what I mean."

She laughed again. "That Bible that you gave me must've had the Holy Ghost itself all over it. I got to reading it last night, and you'll never believe what ended up happening, Jason."

"You heard a choir of angels singing in your room? Is that what happened?"

She was giddy with happiness from having God.talk to her, from having Him touch her. So, she laughed again. "It was something even better. I ain't even gonna put you through guessing. I felt HIM, Jason! I felt God all up in my spirit! He touched me… I know he's real now."

"Well amen then!" Jason almost shouted. He closed his eyes for a few seconds and raised his hand up to Heaven, giving God some praise. That's exactly what he'd been praying would happen for Lisa. He just hadn't expected it to happen so soon. He'd given it a month or two. *But you're a miracle worker, Lord. You hand out some blessings quick and in a hurry. And I thank you for the miracle that you gave the woman I'm falling in love with.*

Jason had known it was going to happen — after all, he knew that the Lord wouldn't allow him to fall in love with a woman who was unable to submit to Him. And by 'Him', he meant God himself.

Jason had been thinking about Lisa ever since he'd woken up that morning. He couldn't get her off his mind. He was really starting to think that she was the soulmate that he'd been praying for for the last two or three years.

"You know that calls for a celebration… Right?" he asked her.

She laughed again. "Like I told you last week, you're really spoiling me, Jason. I really don't know what I'mma do when the Braves season is over with and we're not seeing each other as often."

Jason knew in his heart that he didn't want that to happen — that he didn't want him and Lisa to ever stop seeing each other. She'd barreled into his life like a category five hurricane, and just like a hurricane, she'd left a lasting impression — hers was a good one though.

He smiled into the phone. "Something tells me we're gonna be friends for life, Lisa. Know what I mean?"

She certainly hoped so. But she knew nothing in life was guaranteed.

"About that celebration—," he said, "—Ebenezer hosts a carnival every year — it's pretty similar to the county fair, with rides like the Ferris wheel and even a mini roller coaster. It's going on today. How about I take you there?"

"Oh, yeah. I remember the carnival at Ebenezer. I wanted to go back when I was a teenager, but I never really had the money. Tell you the truth, I had forgotten all about it until you mentioned it just now. But yeah, I'd love to go, Jason."

"Can you be ready in an hour?"

She laughed. "I can be ready in thirty minutes."

Lisa was twenty-five years old — going on twenty-six — but running around with Jason at Ebenezer's carnival made her feel like a kid again. He was a fun guy to hang out with.

Lisa loved the Ferris wheel, so she and Jason had just gotten off their second go around on it. Everything was going just fine – that is until Lisa decided that she wanted some cotton candy. Unfortunately, Tiffany was volunteering at the cotton candy station.

Tiffany could tell that Lisa and Jason were at the carnival together, but since she had every intention of winning Jason over, she resisted the urge to roll her eyes at Lisa when the couple approached her volunteer area. She placed a sweet smile on her face instead.

Tiffany's eyes met Jason's. "Hey, J. I'm surprised you're not volunteering this year." She didn't say a word to Lisa. She acted as if she didn't even exist.

Jason chuckled. "Oh, I'm helping out all right. The carnival doesn't shut down until ten o'clock tonight. My shift starts at five and goes till closing." He smiled. "And I'm pretty much sure that I'm gonna be roped into breaking everything down, too."

Tiffany nodded her head. "Oh, that's right."

The woman who'd led the past two Bible studies — Sister Janet — grinned at Jason and Lisa both. Then she said, "Hang around us long enough, Lisa, and you'll be helping out, too. Next year you'll be standing here with me and Tiffany...getting blue and red food coloring on those pretty little fingers of yours from making cotton candy."

Tiffany nodded her head in agreement. "That's the God knows truth, Sister Janet." Tiffany frowned and looked Lisa dead in the eye. "Hopefully you'll be able to find yourself a way out of whatever charges the Atlanta Police Department put on you a few weeks ago, Lisa. I was watching the eleven o'clock news, and I saw them leading you out of that illegal casino in handcuffs. I prayed for you that night, honey. And I've been praying ever since."

Lisa was well aware that many aspects of her life had been foul up until a few weeks ago, but that didn't mean that she wanted her situation broadcast to half of the people who were in attendance at the carnival. And to make matters worse, Jason's mother had just joined them and Lisa was sure she'd heard Tiffany's catty little statement.

Jason didn't give Lisa the opportunity to respond. He said, "No charges are pending against Lisa, Tiffany. And no charges *will* be pending because none are gonna be filed. You can't prosecute a person if they weren't actually engaged in an illegal activity."

Tiffany pasted an overly bright grin on her face. "Oh, that's good then. What a blessing. I guess the Lord was looking out for you, Lisa."

Jason's mom smiled — a genuine one, unlike Tiffany's. "Most definitely the Lord was looking out for her, Tiffany."

Jason placed his arm around his mother's waist and gave her a quick hug. "Hey, mom, I guess you came over to make sure I'm staying for my shift… Huh?"

Eleanor let out a tiny laugh. "Yep. That's why I made a beeline over here as soon as I saw you. I know you're a very reliable and responsible worker, son, but I noticed that you were having so much fun with Lisa, that

I decided to come and remind you that we're gonna be needing you soon."

"Don't worry, Mrs. Mathis," Lisa said while wearing a grin on her face. "He's already told me that we only have another hour left here and then he's taking me home. But to be honest with you, I don't have anything else planned for today. If you guys need anymore help, I'd be more than happy to volunteer. I understand that the carnival doesn't shut down until ten tonight. I can stay that late… And even later if you need me to."

"Can you, baby?" Eleanor asked.

"Sure."

"Well in that case then, you can start your shift at five — just like Jason. You wouldn't happen to have any face-painting skills would you?"

"Doing custom acrylic nails was a hobby of mine. I had to hand-paint designs — none of those fancy stickers for me. And in high school, I used to think I was gonna be an artist. I can definitely handle face-painting."

Eleanor's grin widened. "Praise the Lord. You can work with me at the face-painting booth. See you there at five."

Tiffany hated hearing that. She'd been volunteering at the carnival for five years and Jason's mom had never once asked her to work directly with her. Now she had another reason to despise Lisa.

Jason and Lisa had about two more hours before they needed to report to their volunteer posts at the carnival. Since the carnival was being held in the spacious parking lot of Ebenezer Christian Center, they decided to go inside of the church — actually one of the waiting rooms — where it was quiet and peaceful and take a break for those two hours.

Lisa pulled out her cellphone and began checking her messages. She was a social media type of sista and she liked staying in the loop. She liked knowing what was going on with her friends and contacts.

Jason pointed at the phone in her hands and smiled. "I guess your phone stays with you wherever you go... Huh?"

Without looking up, she nodded her head. "Yep. Pretty much. But I'm just checking my messages right now. You never know who might need something. Know what I mean?"

Jason knew what she meant all right, but he liked disconnecting himself from social media interactions from time to time. He didn't even have a Facebook account. Nor Twitter. None of that. He was lucky if he checked his text messages once per day. That's just the type of person he was.

"Well," he said, "since you're occupied doing other things, I guess I might as well check my own emails or something."

Lisa was really into reading the notifications on her phone, but she picked up on something in Jason's voice. *It sounds like he's jealous of my phone... Like he wants me to spend all of my time talking to him today.* She had a hard time really believing that, but that's what it kinda seemed like was the case to her. She glanced over at him, and the look on his face kinda-sorta confirmed what she'd been thinking.

*Lemme see something*, she thought to herself. *Lemme see if he cheers up when I put away my phone. If he does, then that means I'm right.*

They were sitting side by side on a comfortable sofa in the waiting room, with their feet up on Ottomans. Lisa slid her cellphone into the pocket of her jeans and leaned back into the sofa cushions. She intentionally let out a very audible sigh and said, "There. All done."

She noticed Jason's face brighten like a light bulb after she'd said that. *He really was jealous of my phone*, she thought to herself. *Or rather, he was peeved that I was spending my time on it instead of talking to him.* That made her think that perhaps he really did like her — maybe as more than just a friend. Then her subconscious mind told her: *You're crazy, boo. He just enjoys spending time with you for some reason. That's all.*

Jason was happy to have Lisa's undivided attention once again. He slipped his cellphone into the pocket of his jeans, too. Then he grinned at Lisa and said, "Ever since I met you, I had this feeling that God had big plans for you, Lisa. Now I'm curious to know what type of plans you have for yourself for the future."

That was an easy one for her. She smiled. "I intend on opening a bakery. My very own bakery. I'm gonna call it *The Real Sweet Spot.*"

"Is that so?"

She gave him a pretend stink eye. "Don't be over there acting like you're surprised that I know how to cook, Jason Mathis."

He laughed. "It's not that, Lisa. You're so fabulous that I just have a hard time imagining you as the domestic type... A hard time imagining you up in a kitchen slinging pots and pans. Know what I'm saying?"

Lisa was notorious for looking fly, so she kind of understood where he was coming from. "I can prove it to you, Jason. You have your own place... If you're willing to open your kitchen up to me after church tomorrow, I'll come over there and bake you something to die for." She paused for a moment then added, "I *would* invite you over to my house for my little bake-off, but you know I'm living with my mama. I don't intend on pushing up on her like that. I don't know what plans she has for her kitchen on tomorrow." *Plus I don't wanna have Jason all up in my mama's face again. She's gonna embarrass me like she did last time — putting us together as a couple and all when Jason's not interested in me like that.*

He didn't have to think about it twice. "You're on, Lisa. And you don't even have to pay for the supplies. I'll pick you up tomorrow and we can go to church together. Then we're gonna hit up the Wally World and get whatever stuff you need." He chuckled. "I'm sure I don't have baking goods at home. I'm a bachelor. I eat out a lot. My fridge and pantry has slim pickings. Only the bare necessities...you know?" He looked her in the eye. "So what are we having for dessert?"

She winked. "It's gonna be a surprise. You'll have to wait and see."

She'd told him to wait and see, but Lisa knew exactly what she wanted to bake for Jason. She'd invented a red velvet cheesecake that was to die for. Unfortunately, it required a springform cupcake pan. Most people didn't exactly have one of those in their kitchen — it was a specialty type of item. Therefore, she told Jason, "We're gonna have to swing by my storage unit first. I have some things in there that I'm gonna need for baking. My storage space is off of East Magnolia Street. That alright with you?"

"Yep. I'll pick you up for church at ten-thirty. As soon as service is over with, we'll swing by the storage center. Then we'll head to Walmart and pick up baking goods and sandwiches from outta that Subway they have in there. My kitchen will be our next stop." He winked his eye. "And if my stomach makes it through your dessert—"

She didn't let him finish his statement. She gave him another pretend stink eye and playfully punched him in his muscular bicep. "Your stomach is gonna be begging for more of my goods, Jason Mathis."

He grinned, then laughed. However, he couldn't help but think to himself that his everything was begging for more of Lisa's goods. He was falling in love with her. He couldn't see how anything but that would be the case.

# CHAPTER 9

Lisa woke up the following morning more than a little excited. She was looking forward to church services that day, as well as the activities that she and Jason had planned for afterward. She loved baking and she suspected that cooking with Jason at his place would be fun. She enjoyed spending time with him.

As for church, if someone had told her a year ago that she was going to actually be excited about attending Sunday morning church services, she wouldn't have believed them. Not at all. She would've said that they were lying. But she was starting to feel a fire in her soul for Christ, so being in a house of God was now her natural inclination. It's where she wanted to be. Where she felt like she needed to be. In her eyes, it was where there was hope and healing.

Lying in bed in her mother's guest room, she sat up and raised her hands towards the heavens. "Thank you God for coming into my life," she whispered. "And thank you for touching a lowly unbelieving little sinner like me." She felt this wonderful sensation in her soul in response to her praise. It was as if God was saying to her: *You're welcome, my child.*

After several seconds of basking in God's glory, she got out of bed and began making preparations for what she was convinced was about to be a wonderful day. *This is the day that the Lord has made*, she thought to herself as she showered. *I shall rejoice and be glad in it.* She didn't know where she'd picked that particular little phrase up from, but she knew that it was true.

*Four Hours Later:*

Joy was shining in Lisa's eyes as she and Jason left Ebenezer Christian Center after services that afternoon. She was still feeling the spirit of the Lord all in her soul — from the top of her head all the way down to the bottom of her feet.

Jason turned on his blinker and pulled out of the parking lot. Then he looked over at Lisa and smiled. "Service was lit today, wasn't it?"

Holding the new Bible that Jason had given her in her lap, Lisa nodded her head in agreement. "It sure was. It was on fire — Holy Ghost fire." She grinned. "I think I'm gonna be ready to answer the altar call real soon. I wanted to go up there and do it today, but at the last minute, my feet didn't move me."

He reached across the center console and gave her hand a gentle squeeze of support. He smiled. "It'll happen for you soon, Lisa. To tell you the truth, I'm, happy to see that you hesitated." Then he quickly added, "Don't get me wrong, I do want to see you walk up to the front of that church and publicly hand your soul over to Christ. But I've seen so many people doing it just to be doing something and not because God had put it on their hearts to. When God tells you to make that step, you'll do it. Just like I did almost a decade ago when I decided to come back into the fold of Christ."

Lisa was encouraged by his words. She had been feeling the same way — meaning that she felt like she'd actually hear a word from God when the time was right for her to offer up her full submission.

It took them less than ten minutes to make it to her storage unit. Jason went with her inside. Seeing her things again made her feel some type of way. She was surprised to notice that she didn't have any type of sadness. Those items represented a life of luxury that she's been living. Yeah it had been tinged with criminal elements, but it had been a comfortable lifestyle.

Lisa placed her hand on her five-thousand-dollar designer sofa, which was now covered in plastic. She knew she wasn't going to miss her old things. They all represented a life that she was happy to have escaped —

even though she was now poor, broke, almost destitute, and living with her mama.

Jason let out a low whistle. "You have some nice stuff in here, Lisa."

"Yeah. I've been thinking about selling most of it at auction or something. I posted a few items online on Craigslist last week. They were snatched up pretty quick. That's how I'm keeping my head above water right now — even though I don't have a job. But I am looking," she quickly tagged on. "I'm not a lazy woman, Jason. I'm more than willing to work hard to sustain myself and get the things I want and need in life."

She'd spent so long being one of Big Ron's kept women that she was surprised to hear herself say that. But she knew it was the truth. From now on, she would be working to get the things she wanted. It would be her, Lisa Denise Washington, putting in the blood, sweat, and tears to achieve her goals.

She knew exactly where the specialty cupcake pan she wanted was located. She made a beeline for it and then she flashed Jason a smile. "You have a mixing bowl and spoon at your house, don't you?"

He chuckled. "Actually, I do. My mom gave them to me one year as a gift."

Lisa laughed. "God bless your mama's little heart. I'm sure you wouldn't have had 'em otherwise." She winked her eye "You're gonna have to work on getting yourself a wife, Jason. She'll make sure you're taken care of."

Lisa didn't know why she'd said that because as soon as the words came out of her mouth, she frowned. She couldn't stop herself. She didn't like imagining Jason married off.

As for Jason, he had a totally different reaction. He smiled. He smiled because he had imagined himself married to Lisa. He liked imagining that.

Without looking at him, she said, "Let's get out of here. The day's wasting away."

Forty-five minutes later, they had everything they needed for the dessert that Lisa had planned for them. They also had foot-long sub sandwiches from the Subway that was located conveniently inside of the Walmart. Lisa had seen Tiffany in there, too. Jason had been reaching up on a high shelf to get a bag of brown sugar for her when Lisa had felt what she had thought was maybe an evil presence around her. She'd turned around and caught a glimpse of Tiffany staring at her from the end of the aisle. Lisa had felt icicles course through her soul from the glare that the girl had been giving her. She was more than happy that Tiffany had decided to keep it stepping instead of coming all the way down the aisle and saying anything to them.

When they rolled into the driveway of a two-story, Mediterranean-style home on the outskirts of Atlanta, Lisa's eyes lit up in approval. She glanced over at Jason and smiled. "Is this you?"

"Yeah. This is the house that I've called home for the last half decade or so. It's quiet out here. Real peaceful. That's why I like it."

Lisa liked it, too. She wouldn't mind living in a house like that. It really was a beautiful home, in an even more beautiful neighbor. The houses weren't piled up on each other like they were in some subdivisions. There was plenty of privacy and the yards were well landscaped. In fact, Jason's spread looked good enough to be in Home and Garden Magazine or something similar.

Lisa smiled. "It's close to that park that you took me to last week, isn't it?"

He nodded his head. "Yep. I didn't think you'd remember. We came over here from the opposite direction when I took you to that park that night. By the way, it's only about a half-mile from here. Not far at all."

As they walked up to Jason's front door with their purchases from Walmart, Lisa couldn't help but comment, "This is a mighty big house for one person to be living in all alone."

"Yeah. It is. When I decided I wanted to stop renting an apartment downtown and buy a house instead, I had the idea of starting a family on my mind. I was twenty-eight back then and figured I was getting old. But as you can tell, God didn't bring my Mrs. Right into my life… Even though I thought I was ready for her."

He had really wanted to say: *God didn't bring her until now*. But for some reason, he didn't feel the timing was right for that. He was waiting for God to lead him on moving forward with Lisa.

Once again, Lisa felt a sadness wash over her from hearing Jason talking about hooking up with a wifey. Why? Because she wanted that position. She wasn't gonna lie to herself about it. She hadn't known Jason for very long, but something within her was telling her that he was her soulmate. Unfortunately, something within her was also telling her that she wasn't qualified to be his wife. It was saying that a girl like herself wouldn't be what he really wanted. Yeah, she'd now found Jesus. But she didn't have the Cosby Show upbringing that Jason had had. Her upbringing had been full of a lot of ghetto drama.

He opened the front door of his home and grinned. "Welcome to my humble home, Lisa. Notw it's showtime. Time to show a brotha what you working with... In my kitchen."

Lisa had to tell herself to get her mind out the gutter again. She'd automatically thought about the bedroom when he'd made his next to last little comment. *Lord give me strength!*

Two hours later, both Lisa and Jason had polished off their sub sandwiches, and the mini red velvet cheesecakes that she'd prepared were in his freezer cooling.

"Based on the way everything smelled while the baking was going on, and based on what those cheesecakes looked like when you took them out the oven, I'm gonna guess that I'm in for a treat, Lisa."

Lisa walked over to his side by side refrigerator and took the cute miniature desserts out of his freezer. "They're ready now, so I guess you're about to see. You gonna owe me some type of compensation since you were laughing and cracking jokes over my baking skills, Jason. What am I gonna get? Huh?"

"I don't know. But I'm sure we can work something out."

He walked over to the kitchen cabinet and took out two saucers and set them on the center island. Lisa proceeded to pop the latches on two of the cups of her springform pan, freeing their dessert. "Prepare those taste buds of yours, Jason. They're about to have a bonafide real treat."

As soon as he placed a forkful of the light and airy concoction into his mouth, Lisa could tell from the look in his eyes that he was enjoying what he was tasting.

She laughed. "Good, ain't it?"

"Baby girl—," using his fork, he pointed at the remaining dessert on his plate, "— this right here is more than good. You got my taste buds sanging... And I do mean *sanging* and not *singing*. Where you learn to cook like this, Lisa?"

"Baking was my hobby when I was growing up."

He placed another forkful in his mouth, this one bigger. "When are you trying to open that bakery of yours?"

She frowned. "It takes big money to do something like that, Jason. I've been mapping out a plan — seeing that I have plenty of time on my hands in between looking for a job. I figure that a cool sixty grand would get me started. I need to find somewhere to lease — you know a kitchen with a storefront attached to work out of. Then I would have to buy equipment and supplies. I don't have that type of cash. Shoot, I'm living in my mama's house."

He suddenly had an idea. "You were talking about putting your things in your storage facility up for auction. I know cars. That Benz that you're rolling around in had to have costed at least a hundred grand new. It looks like it's only about two or three years old. I'm sure you can get at least fifty or sixty grand for it. Of course you'd probably have to sink maybe 10K or so into getting yourself a gently used new car." He smiled. "A sista like yourself can't keep being fabulous if she ain't got no wheels."

Lisa's eyes lit up. She didn't know why she hadn't thought of that. "That's a damn — I mean danggone – good idea, Jason." She'd corrected her language because now that she was in a higher place spiritually, she knew God didn't want her talking like that.

He placed his fork down on his plate. He held out his hands. "Here, let me pray for you on it."

She'd never had anybody offer to pray for her like that. Lisa did indeed feel special now. She held her hands out toward Jason and closed her eyes. She felt all kinds of ways from having her hands in his. But she pushed all that type of thinking aside. Then she allowed him to pray.

When Jason dropped Lisa off at home, it was a little past six in the evening. Lisa had had a great Sabbath. The only dark cloud to her Sunday had been when she'd seen Tiffany down the aisle in the Walmart. She didn't know what to think about the feeling that she'd had when Tiffany had been staring at her.

Lisa was sitting in the living room when her mother came in and asked, "What's troubling you, Lisa? You got this certain look on your face."

Lisa's mother had considered herself saved for the last two or three years or so. Lisa was ready to pick her brain to see if she knew anything about stuff like that.

"Mama, can I ask you something?"

"I can't promise that I'm gonna have the answer. But ask away, baby."

"Have you ever been around somebody and you feel this cold sensation going through your body when you're around them? Now, I'm not talking about feeling cold because it's cold in the room or because it's cold outside. I'm talking about this freezing feeling...just from the way the person is looking at you or something."

Diane frowned and nodded her head. "Tell you the truth, Lisa. I've felt that a time or two — always around people who have a foul, evil spirit about themselves. The last time I felt it, it was Shanika Thompson who caused me to have that feeling. She looked at me a certain way, and I felt like the devil himself had his eyes on me. The next day, she was outside my front window throwing a brick up in my living room — all because she thought I'd been the one talking mess about her. Spreading rumors and whatnot."

Deep in thought, Diane paused for a second. Then she said, "A lot of folk don't realize it, but if you believe in God, you have to believe in Satan. Just like some people have a God spirit in them that's in control, others have a spirit of Satan that's in control. You need to watch out for people like them." She pointed her finger at her daughter in warning. "You hear me, baby?"

Lisa nodded her head. "I hear you, mama."

*Across Town*:

Tiffany finally got home from grocery shopping. She normally didn't buy her groceries at Super Walmart, but she had needed a specific type of pancake syrup and unfortunately, her local Wally World was the only place that she knew sold it. She'd been on an in-and-out run into the store when she'd caught a glimpse of Jason and Lisa in there.

She made her way to her kitchen and pulled a wineglass out her cabinet. After seeing Jason and Lisa together in the store, she figured she was going to need two or three glasses of Chardonnay to calm her nerves.

She poured herself a half glass and got to drinking. "That trick got it all twisted. Ain't no way I'm gonna let her run up in Ebenezer and steal Jason. That shit ain't gonna fly. It ain't flying at all."

She began slipping on her Chardonnay while her brain got to working. Then she suddenly had what she figured was a great idea. She laughed to herself a couple of times as she pulled her cellphone out of her purse. She scrolled down her contacts list to the M section. "I think it's about time for me and Eleanor to have a little chat about Lisa. Eleanor must not realize who we're dealing with. Lisa ain't nothing but a money hungry hoe. I know all about how she was dating Big Ron for his money. Hell, she won't nothing but a well-paid prostitute. I know damn sure Eleanor don't want her son hooking up with nothing like that."

When Eleanor answered her phone and realized that it was Tiffany calling her she was surprised. She had no idea what Tiffany could be possibly reaching out to her for — they didn't have a relationship like that.

"Hello, Tiffany. I hope everything's well with you this evening, dear."

"Everything's just fine with me, Mrs. Mathis. The carnival was real successful yesterday, wasn't it?"

"Yes it was, dear."

"Yeah. We did real good. I guess I better go ahead and get into what I'm calling you for. I don't like gossiping and spreading rumors about people, but I thought you deserved to know about what type of person Lisa Washington really is — seeing how close she seems to be getting with Jason and all."

Eleanor's caution radar began pinging. She hadn't made it to fifty-eight years of age by being stupid. She knew that whenever somebody started a conversation talking about what they didn't like doing, that's the exact thing that they most likely enjoyed doing the most. In other words, she knew beyond a shadow of a doubt that Tiffany was about to call her to gossip and maybe even spread rumors. Eleanor didn't like that. She frowned to herself. I ain't feeling it, but I'm gonna listen to see what angle she's coming from with all of this.

"Alright, Tiffany," Eleanor said. "I understand where you're coming from. Go ahead and speak your piece."

Tiffany launched right into her little exposè about Lisa. Eleanor listened patiently as Tiffany dumped her dirt into her ears.

"So I hope you understand, Mrs. Mathis… That girl can't be nothing but trouble for your son and your family. The Mathises have always been known as upright and decent folk here in the African-American community in

Atlanta. I hate to say it, but Lisa Washington really ain't nothing but a low-class prostitute. I went to school with her — from middle school till high school. She started dating and living with a drug dealer in twelfth grade. From what I understand, she was still living with him and dating him until he got arrested last month. I don't care how much she's pretending like she's a church girl now. I think that's all an act just to get your son for his money. After all, everybody knows that Jason is doing pretty well for himself. He's a catch."

"Wow, Tiffany. I sure do appreciate you thinking enough of Jason and my family to give me this little call of warning."

Tiffany smiled. She knew her call had been a success. Then she said, "Oh, you're very welcome, Mrs. Mathis. Us decent black folk need to learn how to stick together. I'm sure you have plenty of influence over your kids — you're a good mother like that. If you talked to Jason, you could probably get him to change his mind about that girl. Lord knows that's what I would do if I were in your situation. I'd stop low-class heifers like Lisa Washington at my front door."

"Once again, thanks for the heads up, Tiffany."

"Oh, you're more than welcome, Mrs. Mathis."

Tiffany and Eleanor only talked for a few more minutes, and then Eleanor disconnected her phone call. She had a frown on her still-beautiful face as she sat down on the loveseat in her living room. Eleanor hadn't liked the attitude that Tiffany had taken with Lisa because the older woman had already made up in her mind that she liked Lisa. She could tell that her son was falling in love with her, and she could also tell that to the most part, Lisa had a really good heart. *Much better than that lump of coal that Tiffany has in her chest as a heart.*

On top of all of that, Eleanor hadn't always been the upstanding church woman that she now was. In her late teens and early twenties, she too, had lived a questionable lifestyle. Back then, she'd sold dope and turned a few tricks to get the money that she had needed to survive. Fortunately for her, God had sent Jason's father into her life and through a series of events, he'd helped her realize the error of her ways — about like what she knew was going on between Jason and Lisa.

Eleanor's frown deepened. *I'm gonna have to keep my eyes and ears on that Tiffany — make her think we in this here thing together. Something tells me my son is in love with Lisa Washington, and I don't necessarily think that's a bad thing. Lisa might have had a rough start to life, but she got that same look in her eye that I used to have back when I was her age. I can tell she's interested in changing for the better. God wants to use her. I can see the glow all over her.*

Eleanor's husband, Ervin, chose that moment to come into the living room. "Everything alright, sugarplum?" he asked. "You look like you're troubled about something."

143

Eleanor flashed her best friend and lover a smile. "Everything's okay, babe. Everything's gonna be perfectly fine."

# CHAPTER 10

It was now Wednesday, so that meant it had been three days since Lisa had gone to Jason's house to fix dessert for him. She hadn't seen him in person since Sunday, or talked to him on the phone, but he had sent her a few text messages. In fact, he'd texted her every morning wishing her a blessed day. Now, her cellphone was ringing and she realized that it was Jason who was dialing her number.

"Hey, beautiful Lisa. I'm just calling to remind you that we have a date to the Braves game this Friday evening."

She laughed into her phone. "I wouldn't forget about that, Jason. You promised me hot dogs and crackerjacks. I'mma make sure I'm waiting on my mama's front porch on time… Just like I did two weeks ago when we went."

"A'ight. I hear you, girl. You've been doing okay this week, haven't you? You don't need anything, do you?"

Lisa thought it was really sweet of him to ask. She

could tell that his concern was genuine. "I'm doing okay, Jason. Thanks for asking."

They talked for another half hour or so about nothing in particular...they were simply enjoying each other's company over the phone. Then Jason apologized and said that he had to cut their conversation short because he had overshot his break at work by fifteen minutes.

He chuckled into his phone. "Good thing my job is pretty lenient about things like this. I'll see you Friday evening at six o'clock on the nose, sweet Lisa."

After Lisa had disconnected her call with Jason, she thought to herself: *He's gonna have to really stop calling me pet names like that. He's got a sista over here wishing that he really, really did mean them. He got me wishing that I was his girl.*

Since Lisa hadn't seen Carmen in over a week, they were meeting for lunch that day. Carmen had finally found herself a job — one of her ex-highschool teachers had helped her to find it — but she was off today. So the two BFFs decided to take advantage of the time.

Lisa made it to the Mexican restaurant before Carmen did. It's not that Carmen was late, Lisa was just early. When Carmen finally made it to the booth they were sharing she said, "OMG, Lisa! Look at you, boo. You have this glow about yourself, girl."

Lisa smiled. "Oh, do I?" she asked.

Carmen nodded her head. "Yeah. Most definitely. God's sure been working a miracle in you, honey."

"That's what my mama's been saying lately, too."

Carmen chuckled. "What? You don't believe us? You don't believe me and your mama?"

"Oh I believe y'all alright. It's just that I'm working on being humble. Nowadays, when someone gives me a compliment like that, I try not to be all big-headed. Know what I mean?"

Carmen nodded her head in approval. "I definitely understand where you're coming from with that, boo. Humility is a good thing. The Lord enjoys a humble person. It pleases him when we practice humility."

Carmen tilted her head to the side and studied Lisa a little bit more intently. To her, it seemed like there was a little bit more to her girl's glow. She suspected she knew what that something was. "Your friend, Shariece, came into my office yesterday, Lisa. She had wanted to see about enrolling her daughter into our school. We got to talking and she told me that she ran into you at the Walmart on Sunday. She told me it had looked like you had a new boyfriend. That you were laughing, joking, and smiling all up into some fine brotha's face. She said it looked like you were in love." Carmen smiled. "You wouldn't know anything about that, would you?"

Lisa felt such a tight connection with Carmen that she felt like she could tell her almost anything. Plus, she felt like she needed to confide in somebody about how she was feeling. She sighed and said, "I know this is crazy, but I'm pretty much sure that I've fallen in love with Jason."

Carmen grinned. "No, duh? I knew it! I knew you were in love with him! When he took us to church that Sunday, I could tell.. But I didn't want to say anything. I was waiting for you to say something about it first. Plus, I didn't even think you'd realized it yourself yet." Carmen nodded her head. "And the good thing is that he's feeling you, too... He's in love with you."

Lisa frowned. "I don't know about that, boo. I don't think Jason's in love with me. He likes me as a friend — I know that. But love?" She shook her head. "Naw. Nope."

"You're wrong, Lisa. That man loves you, and I want you to put it down on the record that I said so. You see, Jason is an alpha male type of brotha. I'm pretty much sure he's not gonna wait too much longer to tell you how he's feeling about you. Meaning, I know that man is about to stake his claim."

Lisa was certainly praying that Carmen was right, but she doubted it. She didn't feel like talking about that subject anymore. To be honest, it hurt too much. "I think it's time to move on to a different topic, Carmen. Speaking of Jason and me being in the Walmart last weekend, I saw Tiffany while I was in there. And you should've seen the way that she was looking at me.

Girrrrl... I swear I felt an evil vibe coming off of her... And she was all the way at the end of the aisle."

"Lord, Lisa...I'm glad you brought her up." Carmen pointed a finger of warning at her bestie. "You need to keep an eye on that heifer. You hear me? I had a dream last night about her butt. In my dream, she had this big ol' knife over your head — it was a machete or something. I'm pretty much sure that God was trying to tell me that that girl is dangerous, and for whatever reason she's gonna be gunning for you. So keep your eyes open, boo. Watch your back."

That's the very same message that Lisa had gotten from her conversation with her mother on the subject. She took Carmen's dream as confirmation that she need to be extra careful where Tiffany was concerned.

Carmen sighed then said, "Now that we got that out the way... Are there any developments in your job hunting efforts?"

Lisa finally smiled again. "Not really. But I think I done made some lead-way towards making an employment opportunity for myself."

"For real?"

"Yep. I was talking to Jason the other day and he put this real good idea in my head." Lisa's eyes began shining in excitement. "I'm selling the Benz, girl, and using the money to open that bakery I was telling you about."

Carmen grinned, too. "That's a good idea, Lisa. I'm

sure you can get at least fifty or sixty grand for that car. I wonder why we didn't think about that."

"I know… Right?"

*Downtown at the Police Station:*

Jason finally made it upstairs to his sixth floor office. His co-worker, Jermaine, grinned as Jason came in and took a seat behind his desk.

"You're not normally the one coming in late from your breaks, Jason." He chuckled. "It's usually me doing that. That pretty young thang you been running around with had you caught up, didn't she?"

Jason wasn't gonna deny it. He smiled, too. "Real talk, bruh, I'd spend all my time with Lisa if I could."

Jermaine chuckled again. "Sounds like she got you sprung, Jason."

He wasn't ashamed of how he felt for the woman who had stolen his heart. He was too thankful that God had sent his soulmate into his life for all of that. He felt blessed. "Yeah, I'm sprung all right, Jermaine."

"Sounds like I'm about to have to rent myself a tux for a wedding."

Thinking about Lisa being his bride and wife, Jason smiled. "I hope so, bruh. I haven't even told her how I feel about her yet. But I intend on doing all of that real soon. I've been praying on it, and last night, God gave me the go-ahead."

"He did?"

"Yep. I 'd said my prayers before going to bed — like I normally do — and as soon as I opened my eyes, I heard a voice in my head saying: *Tell her how you feel.*"

Jermaine wasn't exactly living a saved lifestyle, but he knew about God and his goodness. "That was definitely God that you heard, bruh." He grinned. "I guess I *will* be renting that tux."

Jason thought so, too. In fact, he knew so. Now he could barely wait to see Lisa's beautiful face again — which was gonna be in two days at the Braves game.

Lisa's eyes were shining with excitement as soon as Jason helped her into the passenger side seat of his SUV. Jason got behind the wheel and backed out of the driveway, then he glanced over at her and smiled. "You got a shine in your eyes, Lisa. What are you so excited about?" Then he added, "And I know it's not the game we're about to go to — even though they're your team. That look in your eye says that it's something bigger."

She giggled. "You didn't see the Benz in the driveway when you drove up, did you?"

He had indeed noticed that it hadn't been there, but

he hadn't really given it too much thought. He'd been too busy thinking about how beautiful Lisa was, and how much he loved her. Now it suddenly hit him. As realization dawned, he grinned, too. "You sold it, didn't you, sweetheart?"

She was too excited herself to notice the term of endearment that he'd just dropped...to notice that he'd just called her sweetheart.

She bobbed her head up and down. "I sure did. And for a good price, too. That car had all of the upgrades that were being offered on the day that I bought it. You and I were thinking that I was only gonna get fifty or sixty grand for it. I actually got sixty-three! I know it won't nothing but a blessing straight from God himself." She raised her hand towards the ceiling and shouted, "Hallelujah!" Then she grinned and said, "I had thought it was gonna take me several weeks to get it sold." She snapped her fingers. "But it happened...just like that."

He reached across the center console and took her hand into his. He gave it a gentle squeeze. "I'm so happy for you, babe."

With him holding her hand like he was, Lisa actually noticed the term of endearment this time. *He called me babe.* She couldn't stop the feeling of male–female awareness from making a quick rush through her body. She was definitely attracted to Jason, and since she was in love with him, him calling her babe had triggered that feeling.

While she was sitting there happy but confused, he continued speaking. "Congratulations. That blessing of yours was the best news I've heard all day."

He squeezed her hand one more time, then placed both of his hands on the steering wheel to navigate the tight Atlanta traffic on the interstate.

They of course enjoyed their time at the ballgame. When the Braves wrapped up their win against the Astros, Jason and Lisa made their way out of SunTrust Park — which is where the Braves home field was located.

He looked across his SUV at her and smiled. "Wanna go walk our ballpark food off, Lisa?"

For some reason she suddenly felt shy around him. She simply smiled and nodded her head yes.

Twenty minutes later, they were sitting on the same park bench as last time, gazing up at the stars. Jason lifted his lips in a tiny smile and said, "A whole lot has happened for you in the two weeks since we were last here. You accepted Christ into your life, you came up with a game plan to make your bakery dream a reality, and you sold your car — which is gonna finance The Real Sweet Spot."

She nodded her head in agreement. "Yeah. But a whole lot of that has to do directly with you, Jason. I wanna thank you for being on Team Lisa... For supporting me like you have, you know?" She sighed. "Even though I should've thought about it, I don't think it would've occurred to me that I should sell my car. You helped me realize that." She smiled and continued speaking. "The Benz was nice, but I'm not connected to material things like I used to be. So letting it go didn't even hurt. And what I got in exchange — a chance to open my bakery — was well worth it." Her eyes met his. "So thank you, Jason."

He took her hand into his again. "You're welcome, sweetheart."

*There he goes again. He's calling me sweetheart.*

She fixed her lips to question him about him addressing her that way, but before she could say anything, he said, "I wasn't gonna tell you this until later, but I think I might have found you the perfect place to put your bakery. There's a nice bakery downtown that I've been going to for years. I know the owner pretty well. He's retiring soon. He's willing to sale you all of the equipment in his bakery shop at a discount, and I'm sure the people who actually own the building will jump at the chance to quickly get a new lessee in there." He grinned. "Nobody wants a rental property sitting empty for an extended amount of time. You can't make money like that."

Her eyes lit up again. "For real, Jason? Are you for real?"

"Yeah, girl."

He chuckled and stood up. "We can do a quick drive-by right now. Seeing that you don't have a car, I can pick you up tomorrow at noon during my lunch break and we can take a peek at the inside. That sound good to you?"

Yep, she was all for that.

*Twenty Minutes Later:*

Just from peeking on the inside, Lisa could tell that the bakery that Jason had brought her to would be the perfect home for *The Real Sweet Spot*.

With her face pressed to the ground-to-roof picture glass window, Jason asked, "Well, what do you think? Did I call it or what?"

She pulled back slightly from the window and smiled and nodded her head. "You called it all right, Jason Mathis. I can imagine it already. This place is perfect."

She'd been smiling — that is up until now. Now she frowned.

Her change in demeanor wasn't lost on Jason. "What's wrong, Lisa?"

She sighed. "Um, well, I had money and everything back when I was with Big Ron, but I wasn't real good at handling it. Well, I was okay with handling it, I just didn't like paying my bills on time. I thought I was too good for something like that. Of course I know better now, but I think that my past behavior is about to come bite me in the butt." She shook her head. "What I'm trying to say is that my credit is messed up, Jason. It's messed all the way up...especially now. With no income, I haven't been able to pay some of my credit card bills that I owe. My credit is bad — and when I'm talking bad, I mean *really* bad. Ain't nobody gonna let me lease no building with credit like I got. And I don't know anybody who has decent credit who could lease it for me... Or cosign on the lease."

He smiled. Then using his thumb and forefinger, he tilted her chin and looked directly into her eyes. "I have excellent credit, Lisa. I'll cosign on this storefront. I'll even lease it entirely in my name if you need that to happen."

In the whole time she had known him, Jason had been a man of his word. If he had told her he was going to do something, he did it. That's one of the things she liked most about him.

With her eyes staring into his, she asked, "Why would you do a thing like that for me, Jason. You've only known me about a month."

He knew the time was right. He knew it was time to let the beautiful woman standing in front of him know how he was feeling about her. He placed his palm against her soft cheek and smiled. "I take care of the people I love, Lisa. I'm in love with you, girl. It doesn't matter to me that I've only known you a month… My heart feels like it's known you forever."

"What?"

He grinned and nodded his head. "Yeah. I'm in love

with you. You ran up into my life and stole my heart, Lisa."

She hadn't been expecting to hear him say any of that. Not at all. She was in love with him, too, and she knew it. However, based on her prior beliefs in boss chicks like herself never giving away their hearts, she wasn't ready to admit to him.

Jason understood Lisa without her even saying a word. He didn't get upset about her not immediately confessing her love for him — he knew that was going to take her a little bit more time. But he knew how she felt about him. In her eyes, she carried the same look of love that he had for her — he'd seen it.

He smiled again. "I know a confession of love from me is kinda sudden. But God put it on my heart that it was okay for me to let you know how I was feeling about you. We can take things slow — meaning we can start by dating. But I'm putting you on notice, Lisa... I know there's gonna be an us. I know you're that soulmate I've been praying for, girl. God's already shown me that."

Her heart was telling her that she was in love with him, too — it had been telling her that. Now that everything was out in the open, it was a little scary. But something inside of her was saying: *Go ahead and take him up on his offer. Dating is a good place to start.*

She finally smiled. "I think I'd like it if we could start with dating, Jason."

# CHAPTER 11

Carmen looked across the restaurant that she and Lisa were having dinner in and grinned. "Now that you and Jason are officially a couple, I hardly ever get to see you, girl. I'm getting a little jelly."

Just hearing Jason's name mentioned brought a smile to Lisa's face. "Boo, that boy is something else. I really do enjoy spending time with him, Carmen."

Carmen nodded her head. "That's because you're in love with him, honey. And the two of you look so stinking cute together... Everybody thinks so." A frown made its way onto her face. "Everybody but Tiffany. Something's wrong with that girl. I mean seriously wrong. I wasn't gonna say anything to you, but I'm your bestie, so I think I need to." Carmen's frown deepened and she continued speaking. "Tiffany's been spreading rumors about you to anybody who would listen. I was talking to Tundra Peeler the other day, and she told me that Tiffany had told her that you had had eleven abortions." Carmen shook her head. "I know that was a lie because you're my girl. I'm pretty much sure you would've told me if you'd had even one. Then she told Keisha Johnson that you were making money right now by doing pornos."

"What?"

Carmen nodded her head. "Yep. Keisha told me that yesterday."

The old Lisa would've been done called Tiffany out for her duplicitous behavior. There wouldn't have just been words exchanged between the two either. Oh no to that, Lisa would've been ready to fight. Truth be told, she was ready to fight right now. She wanted to make her way over to Tiffany's house, ring her doorbell, and punch her in the face as soon as she opened her front door. *Right after that, I'd tell her to keep my name out her mouth. But that ain't the way I roll now. I'mma let God fight this battle for me.* She frowned. *At least I hope I'm gonna let you fight it, Lord. I'm itching to hand out some street-style justice. I wanna put my foot all up that tricks as—, uh, I mean butt.*

Lisa took a sip from her glass of tea. "I'm gonna leave Tiffany in God's hands, Carmen. Just keep praying for me, girl, cause you know the struggle is real. I'm really trying not to, but my urge to lay hands on her trifling behind is getting real strong."

Carmen nodded her head in understanding. "You stay in my prayers, boo. To me you're family. I don't have any other choice."

# STUMBLING INTO A PRAYER

*Over at Jason's House:*

Jason had gotten home from work two hours ago. He'd just finished eating his meal of Chinese takeout and now he was sitting in front of the television in his mancave about to catch a movie. He really wanted to give his baby a call — he wanted to talk to Lisa. But since he knew she was having a girls' night out with her bestie, he decided not to go there.

When someone began ringing his doorbell, he had Lisa on his mind. A big part of him was hoping that it was her at his door, but the rational-thinking part of his brain was telling him that wouldn't be the case — that she was still out on the town enjoying herself with Carmen. When he looked out his peephole, he frowned. One of the last people he was expecting to be there was staring him in the face.

He pulled his door open and said, "Hey, Tiffany. What's up?"

Tiffany smiled. "Hey, Jason. I would've called first, but God put it on my heart to drive over here and show you what I need to show you in person."

Jason couldn't imagine what Tiffany could possibly need to show him. He frowned and said, "What do you need to show me, Tiffany?"

She looked around his solidly-built body and into his

living space. "Um, can I come in? I don't think you're gonna want to see this while we're standing out here on your front porch. It's a little too personal. It's about Lisa—," she frowned, "—you know, the Lisa you been running around with lately."

Despite him not really wanting to let Tiffany into his home for some reason, hearing her mention Lisa's name prompted him to open his door a little wider and allow Tiffany to step inside his most private place.

Tiffany strutted in like she was a boss, like she owned things. She took a seat on his spacious sofa. Then she whipped her cellphone out her purse. She looked him in the eye. "I don't bite, Jason... Not unless you want me to. Come have a seat. What I need to show you is here on my cellphone."

Jason sat down beside her and took the phone that she had handed him. A frown jumped on his face when he caught a glimpse of the video that she was playing. He could tell that it was a porno flick. And what was even worse, a girl who looked like his baby was the main star.

He looked at the video for several seconds, then he handed the phone back to Tiffany. "Is that all you came over here to show me?"

She nodded her head. "Pretty much. I'm sorry I had to show you this and all, Jason. But you're a good person. You're a strong, God-fearing type of brotha...a real man of God...a man of morals and convictions. Hooking yourself up with a girl like Lisa ain't gonna do nothing but get you hurt. That video that you just saw was recorded this year — last month really. And before you even ask, I checked into it. The filming date that I just quoted you is legit."

She stood up from her perch on his sofa, then she bent down and placed her palm against Jason's cheek. "I'm sorry you had to see that, boo. I really am, and I'm here for you if you need someone to talk to after you shut Lisa down…"

She leaned into his ear and whispered. "I've always had a soft spot in my heart for you, Jason." She stood up straight. "I'm gonna go ahead and get on up out of here. Like I told you, God put it on my heart to show you that. He put it in my spirit."

"I know you have my cell number… Can you text me a copy of the video, Tiffany?"

She smiled in satisfaction. She was sure he was about to go confront Lisa with it and she knew a break up for them was sure to follow. "Sure, Jason. As soon as I get in the car."

As soon as he heard his front door close behind Tiffany, Jason pushed his head back into the cushions of his sofa. A deep frown now seemed to be a permanent fixture on his face.

*Two Hours Later*:

Lisa hadn't been expecting Jason to come visit her that night, but yet here he was standing on her mother's doorstep at ten twenty-five.

She flashed him a smile as she stepped out the front door. "Hey, babe. You missed seeing me so much today that you just had to come over and visit?"

Her grin disappeared with a quickness when she caught a glimpse of the look on his face. She grimaced. "What's wrong, Jason?"

"Come sit in the truck with me Lisa. I need to show you something."

She could tell that this something was pretty serious. She nodded her head and followed him to his vehicle. He got her car door like he'd been doing ever since they'd first met. When he was settled behind the steering wheel, he handed her his phone with the video playing. He only allowed it to run for about fifteen seconds, then he took the phone from out of her hands and shut the video off.

Lisa was shocked. She frowned and her eyes met his. "That wasn't me, Bae. You gotta believe me. That girl might look like me, but it wasn't."

He surprised her by saying, "I know it wasn't you, sweetheart. I always felt like that saying about everybody having a twin out there somewhere was true."

She felt relief flooding over her. She didn't know what she would've done if Jason hadn't believed her.

He sighed. "What's troubling me about all of this is

the way that Tiffany rolled up into my place and showed me this. God put it on my heart that she doesn't mean you — and she doesn't mean us — any good. She's jealous of you, babe, and her jealousy is outta control. I could tell that from the look I saw in her eyes. I'm a police detective. I've seen it many times in hardened criminals before they committed crimes of passion."

Lisa considered herself to be a babe in Christ, but her faith and belief were strong. She took Jason's hand into hers. "God's got my back in whatever foulness Lisa could ever cook up. I was talking to Carmen about Tiffany and her shenanigans over dinner tonight. I came home and prayed on it for a long time. God kept giving me the same thought in my mind after I had prayed. And that thought was: *No weapon formed against me shall prosper.*

She sucked her teeth. "I ain't scared of that trick. Like I said: *Jesus is the captain of Team Lisa.*

*Across Town*:

Tiffany pulled out her phone because she'd just received a new text message. She smiled when she realized that it was from Angela.

Angela: *Did you do it?*

164

Tiffany: *Yeah*

Angela: *What did he say?*

Tiffany: *He asked me 2 text him a copy. U shoulda seen look on his face. Lisa ass outta here. He dumping her. I know he is.*

Angela: *LOL!*

TIffany: *Yeah LOL.*

<<<<◇>>>>

*A Week Later*:

Holding hands with Jason, Lisa stood in the center of the bakery that was now all hers. The previous owner had been itching to retire. As soon as Lisa had offered him thirty-nine grand for all of his equipment and furniture, he'd shut his doors and taken the money and run.

Lisa felt like crying. "I can't believe all of this is mine, Bae. I just can't believe it. And thank you again for signing the lease to rent it. My credit was messed up... I wouldn't be standing in here right now if you hadn't done that."

Jason gave her hand a tiny squeeze. Then he released her hand and wrapped his arms around her waist instead. He placed a soft kiss on her lips. Next, he pulled back and smiled. "You're welcome, sweetheart. Like I told you a few weeks ago... I love you, Lisa. I'd do almost anything to see you prosper."

Having the man she loved holding her in his arms like that was wrecking havoc to Lisa's self-control. She considered herself to be saved now, but she was a grown woman who had grown woman needs and urges. Jason was fine in every way. She felt like jumping his bones, and she was constantly praying to God and asking him to keep her urges under control.

"What's wrong, Bae?" he asked.

She didn't feel like telling him the truth — that she felt like taking him into the back room of her new bakery and sensually showing him how much she loved him. She figured that would be inappropriate.

Jason leaned into her ear and whispered, "I feel the same way... It's a natural feeling when a man and woman love each other like we do. You know neither one of us would have to keep suffering like this if you went ahead and agreed to marrying me. I'm sure you could throw us together a fabulous wedding on short notice. Say you'll be my wife, Lisa. With God as my witness...I love you, girl."

Her lips spreaded into a slow smile, then she was surprised by the tears that sprang into her eyes. She loved

166

Jason so much.

She nodded her head. "I love you, too, Jason. Yes, I'll become your wife!"

He shouted out in victory. Then he picked her up in his arms and swung her around in circles a few times. With joy shining in his eyes, he kissed her again — this kiss was full of all the passion and love that he carried in his heart for her. "Thank you, babe. You just made me the happiest brotha in town."

Jason had wanted to announce their engagement to their parents at the same time, so he'd invited Lisa's mom and his own parents out to dinner at Red Sizzler on Friday night. Lisa liked Jason's mom and she suspected that Mrs. Mathis liked her too. But on account of her upbringing and previous lifestyle, Lisa wasn't sure that the woman would want her as a daughter-in-law. Since she tended to discuss almost everything with Carmen, Lisa gave her girl a call on Thursday evening.

"Hey, boo. It's me."

Carmen smiled into her phone. "I know it's you, Lisa. I got caller ID... Remember? What's up?"

Lisa sighed, then she smiled. "Jason asked me to marry him and I said yes."

Carmen laughed. "Congratulations, honey. It's about danggone time." Then she realized that something was off. "What's wrong, Lisa? There's something troubling about the tone of your voice. You're about to marry the love of your life… It seems like you should be a little happier than that."

Lisa shook her head. "It's his folks, boo. I'm not sure they're gonna want me marrying their son...especially not his mama."

"Why would you say something like that? I've seen you and his mama together. It seemed like she liked you to me. Shoot, she knew y'all were dating and she didn't protest. She ain't stupid. I'm sure she knew that Jason was in love with you and that he was gonna eventually ask you to marry him. It ain't like he's a worldy type of brotha. He wouldn't just keep a girlfriend indefinitely."

Lisa frowned. "But his family is like the freaking Cosby Show. His mama could be Claire Huxtable's clone."

"Lisa, you need to quit and stop worrying about nothing, honey. Like I said, that woman likes you — I'm sure she can tell that you have a really good heart and you really love her son. She ain't about to be upset about you marrying Jason." Carmen chuckled. "Shoot, she ain't got no grandkids yet. She probably ready to pay you to marry him just about now and start pushing out some babies."

The next day at the dinner that Jason had set up, Lisa realized that her girl had been right. As soon as Jason had announced their engagement, Eleanor Mathis jumped out of her chair and did a Holy Ghost happy dance right there in the restaurant. She pulled Lisa into her arms for a warm hug as soon as she was finished. Then she whispered into her ear, "Welcome to the family, honey."

Lisa could do nothing but grin and say, "Thank you."

# CHAPTER 12

Based on Jason's reaction to the video that she'd shown him a week and a half ago, Tiffany had been convinced that Jason and Lisa were going to be breaking up. When she saw them stroll into church holding hands, she couldn't stop the look of shock and disappointment from coming onto her face.

Her shock and disappointment morphed into anger when Sister Janice got up to give the church announcements for the week. The woman stood behind the podium and asked the church to congratulate Jason and Lisa on their engagement. She'd said that the happy couple intended on tying the knot at the end of the following month.

The church was serving dinners after service in the fellowship hall, and Tiffany was supposed to be helping. But she was so upset about that announcement that she decided she wouldn't be contributing her time and efforts after all.

170

Tiffany was leaving early from services when she heard Lisa's voice in the ladies room. She didn't go in. She decided to stay outside and eavesdrop.

Lisa and Carmen stood at the long counter with triple sinks and washed their hands. Lisa smiled at her bestie and said, "Thanks for coming here to Ebenezer today to give me moral support when they announced me and Jason's engagement, boo. I don't know why I was so nervous about everything. But it was good having you here."

Carmen grinned, too. "You're welcome, honey. You know I'm always gonna have your back... Right?"

Lisa nodded her head, prompting Carmen to continue speaking. "That's why I'm telling you right now that I'm concerned about you not going ahead and buying insurance for your bakery. That's an almost fifty-thousand-dollar investment that you're dealing with, girl. If something happens over there — like a fire or a natural disaster — your butt is toast. You gonna be up the creek without an oar."

Lisa sighed. "I know, boo. I needed transportation, so after I paid for the equipment, I used most of the money that was left over from selling the Benz to buy that Jeep Grand Cherokee that I was telling you about. It's used, but it still costed me a little over ten grand. I *do* need reliable transportation to get around in. Know what I'm saying? Unfortunately, because of my credit and everything, the insurance company had wanted five grand upfront to open up a decent policy for me. But don't worry though. I'm selling some of the stuff that I still have in storage. I think I should have the money by next week. I don't think anything is gonna happen to my bakery between then and now. The chances of that are what—," she paused, "—one in a billion?"

Standing outside the door to that ladies room, a hateful, devious little smile made its way onto Tiffany's face. As she walked out the exit doors of the church, she felt like dancing. *That trick is about to pay now.*

Lisa looked around her bakery and smiled. She was amazed at everything that God had blessed her with. The bakery had been in pretty good shape when she'd bought it from Jason's friend. All she'd had to do was some minor cosmetic changes — things like adding a little bling and sparkle here and there — basically adding her personal style and touch, thus making it her own.

She had enough recipes in her repertoire that she wasn't worried about the goodies she was going to be selling. And the part-time job that she'd had at a bakery during high school had given her some experience.

She turned around, looked at Jason and smiled. "Well, Bae. What do you think?"

He wrapped his arms around her waist. "I think you're absolutely beautiful, Lisa."

She shook her head but grinned. "I'm talking about what do you think about the bakery. Not about me, sweetheart."

"Oh."

"Well?"

"It's fly… Just like you. You have a good eye for fashion and detail, Bae. The Real Sweet Spot is gonna be the dopest and best bakery in town. Everybody is gonna love it. I've tried all of your recipes. They're gonna love your food, just like I do."

Lisa knew that she'd done a good job on the interior of her place, and she knew her desserts were on point, but that still didn't mean that she wasn't a little nervous. She sighed. "I'm praying that everybody likes it, Jason."

He dropped a soft kiss on her lips. "They will. In two weeks when you open up, you'll see." He winked his eye. "And four weeks after that, when we get married, you'll also get to see and experience how very, very much *I* love you."

She knew exactly what he was talking about and that made Lisa blush. They both took their salvation seriously, so premarital sex wasn't something that was in the cards for either of them.

However, feeling kind of flirtatious, she winked her eye at him. "I think you're gonna be the one who's in for an experience Mr. Mathis."

She was glad that his cellphone began ringing at that point because things were starting to get kind of steamy between them. The sexual tension was off the charts.

"Lord, give me strength," she whispered under her breath as her man went to take his phone call.

Five hours later, it was a little past eleven at night when Lisa received a phone call from the Atlanta Fire Department.

Still a little drowsy, she bolted straight up in bed. "Come again... What did you just say?"

"There's been a fire at your bakery, ma'am. It's pretty bad...it looks like you lost everything. You're gonna probably wanna make your way on over here to survey the damage. Most insurance companies have adjusters on the clock twenty-four seven. You're probably gonna want to call your insurance provider so they can come over, too."

As soon as Lisa disconnected her call, she wanted to cry. She didn't have insurance. She'd planned on signing up for a policy in a few days after her money had cleared from selling some of the furniture in her self-storage unit.

"The impossible happened, Lord. I'm screwed. My hopes and my dreams just went up in smoke."

*An Hour Later*:

Lisa really did cry when she took a look at what remained of her yet-to-open bakery. She didn't need anyone to tell her that it was a complete loss.

Jason placed his arms around his baby and allowed her to cry on his broad shoulder. He patted her back and said, "I know it looks bad, but it's gonna be alright, sweetheart. The insurance company will take care of all of this."

She shook her head. She felt like such an idiot. A fool. "No they're not."

"Yes, they are, Lisa."

She'd never snapped at Jason before, but she was so distraught that she did now. "I said, no, they're not!"

He didn't take offense from her tone of voice. Given the situation, he kinda sorta understood. He pulled back from their embrace and tilted her chin up so that he could look her directly in the eye. He chanced a tiny smile. "The insurance company is gonna pay for this, Lisa."

"I don't have insurance," she finally cried out. Then the floodgates to her tears really busted open.

Wanting to comfort his fianceè, he pulled her back into his arms, and she allowed him to do it. She didn't fight him at all.

He leaned into her ear and began whispering. "You *do* have insurance, babe. *We* have insurance. I figured that you wouldn't exactly have the money to take care of that — seeing that they wanted a five thousand dollar deposit upfront and all. But since my name's on the lease here, they allowed me to get insurance. I went ahead and opened *The Real Sweet Spot* a policy. Everything's covered, Bae. You're gonna get your money back for everything that was damaged tonight and we're gonna rebuild. You hear me, sweetheart?"

She couldn't believe what he was saying, even though she knew that Jason had never lied to her before. With tears in her eyes, she pulled back and studied his face. She could tell that he was telling her the truth.

He grinned even harder. "You believe me now, don't you?"

She smiled, too. "Yeah. Thank you, Jason... And sorry for almost biting your head off a few minutes ago."

He pulled her into his arms again for another hug. "I'll let you apologize properly on our wedding night in a few weeks," he whispered into her ear.

Lisa liked that idea. She was definitely up for that.

*The Following Morning:*

Jason's mother, Eleanor, had invited Lisa over to her home for breakfast, so Lisa was sitting at his mother's kitchen table when she received a call from her fianceè.

"Are you sure about that, Jason? Arson? The fire detective told you that someone intentionally set that blaze at my bakery?"

Because of his position as a police detective, Jason had connections with various officials downtown. Within an hour of the investigation at The Real Sweet Spot being completed, he had a copy of the official report on his computer screen.

He frowned, then he switched his cellphone over to his other ear. "Yeah. I'm positive. I looked at the report with my own two eyes. Then I called and spoke with the chief detective at the fire department for confirmation. There was an accelerant involved in the blaze — that's why it got so hot so fast. It was most likely gasoline. It was an act of arson and I've started the paperwork to initiate a criminal investigation."

"Dang. That's messed up."

"Yeah. Listen, babe...do you know anybody who would've wanted to burn you out like that?"

Lisa hadn't exactly been a choir girl before meeting Jason, so she knew it was a few people that she'd had beef with. But she hadn't necessarily done anything so terrible that any of them would've been gunning for her like that.

She frowned. "I don't know who would've done me like that, Jason."

Lisa and Jason talked for only a minute or so longer, then they disconnected their call. Lisa turned to her future mother-in-law and grimaced. "Did you catch that, Mrs. Mathis?"

Eleanor frowned. "Yeah. I sure did, and I think you and Jason need to add Tiffany Scott's name to the top of y'all's suspect list. That girl is pure evil and she don't like you, baby. She's had her eye on Jason for years, and you rolled up in here and snatched him up. You stole his heart—," she snapped her fingers, "—just like that, and Tiffany don't like it."

"But it wouldn't make sense for her to burn my shop down. Most people have insurance and they replace whatever is lost."

Eleanor shook her head. "She knew you didn't have insurance, Lisa. I heard her talking to Angela at choir rehearsal yesterday. She told Angela that you were a stupid b-word who was too dumb to get insurance after spending fifty grand on opening a business. She said something about hearing you tell Carmen that this past Sunday at church." Eleanor frowned. "Then she said it would be funny if a fire or something similar came through and destroyed your bakery."

Lisa had already explained her insurance situation to her future mother-in-law that morning. But she was still embarrassed because not having insurance was ridiculous — even though at the time she figured it was for a good reason and she had planned on opening up a policy real soon.

Eleanor smiled and patted Lisa's hand. "Don't worry, we all make mistakes honey. It's a good thing that my son's a good man and he had your back."

Lisa nodded her head in agreement. "Yeah. Lord knows that's the truth."

"You see why I think Tiffany did it, don't you?"

"Yeah. As payback. I think you might be right, Mrs. Mathis."

"Go ahead and call my son, baby. Tell him about what we think."

Less than a minute later, Jason was nodding his head in agreement as Lisa explained to him exactly why she thought that Tiffany should be elevated to the number one suspect position.

Jason frowned as he pinched his chin between his thumb and forefinger. "I think you and my mama are right, Bae. I know you remember how I told you that it was Tiffany that showed me that porno flick of that girl who looked like you. If she would do something like that to try to eliminate you as competition, it's easy to believe that she would do something like set your shop on fire when she thought you didn't have insurance… You know, as payback and to hurt you because you had something that she wanted. To hurt you because you have me."

He nodded his head. "I'll definitely be placing her name in the number one suspect slot. Well, I won't be doing it—," he corrected himself, "—because it's not my case. But I'll be talking to the person who's handling it, and I'll be keeping daily tabs on the case's progress. We're gonna get whoever did this, Bae. We're gonna lock 'em up. You can trust and believe that."

After Lisa had completed her call, Eleanor gave her a satisfied smile. "Jason's good at what he does. I know he's not gonna allow the fool — who would do something like this to the woman he loves — get away. If Tiffany Scott committed this crime — like I think she did — she's gonna be serving some hard time. My son's gonna make sure the book's thrown at her when she gets her day in court."

Ten days had passed and the authorities couldn't find any evidence whatsoever to connect anyone to the arson at Lisa's bakery. Lisa and Jason were supposed to be getting married in four short weeks. But instead of focusing on her wedding, Lisa was worrying about the crime that had been committed against her and getting her business back together.

Sitting on his sofa, she laid back in Jason's arms. "I just don't believe that they're still turning up nothing on my case."

Jason sighed. "I know, Bae. But unfortunately, I think a professional had a hand in this — someone who is used to covering up their tracks."

"So you don't think that Tiffany did it anymore? I can't imagine her being a professional at committing arson."

"Well, what I suspect is that she hired someone to do it."

"Feel free to tell me that what I'm about to say is

ridiculous, but I was talking to your mama this afternoon and she dropped an idea in my head. She told me that you and I should pretend that we broke up and you should make nice with Tiffany. Once she thinks you're on her team, your mama said that she'll probably confess — she said that's the way that women like Tiffany are."

It sounded like something out of a soap opera, but Jason figured that it could possibly work. Nothing else was working so far and they were passing the time window of the case being hot.

He frowned. ""But we'd have to postpone our wedding, babe."

"I don't mind that Jason. It would be worth it to me if we caught Tiffany." She shrugged her shoulders. "Plus, before getting saved, I considered myself to be a real boss chick. Which meant that I didn't think I'd ever get married anyway. It's not like I grew up with big dreams of having a wedding. If you're for it, I think we should give your mama's idea a shot."

She looked him in the eye. "You down or what, Bae?"

He nodded his head. Then he gave her a fist bump. "I'm down."

She smiled. "That's what I'm talking about. Just don't be kissing her all in the mouth when you start getting friendly with her...you feel me?"

He chuckled and proceeded to give Lisa a sensual kiss on her lips. Then he pulled back and grinned.

"You're the only woman I wanna think about kissing, babe. My tongue is reserved all for you."

She held out her hands. "Let's pray on everything, Jason. I don't like having to try to trap Tiffany like this, but let's put God's covering on our actions. Even King Solomon from the Bible had to practice the art of war, and we're definitely at war with Tiffany if she set my bakery on fire."

Jason loved the way his woman brought God into everything she did in her life. He felt blessed to have her by his side.

# CHAPTER 13

Tiffany couldn't stop smiling when Angela told her that the word going around the church was that Lisa and Jason had called off their wedding and broken up.

"Who told you that they weren't together anymore, boo?" she asked Angela as they talked over the phone.

"I heard his mama telling Sister Janice at choir practice. She said it won't no way they were getting back together. Something about him rethinking his position on some video she was in."

The video that she'd shown Jason several weeks ago popped up into Tiffany's mind — the porno flick that starred a girl that looked just like Lisa.

A little birdie had told Tiffany that Jason liked having coffee at the Starbucks in the mall on Friday mornings — his day off. She smiled to herself. *Tomorrow's Friday. I'm gonna be in that Starbucks. Hopefully, he'll show up.*

# STUMBLING INTO A PRAYER

*The Following Morning*:

Jason wasn't exactly surprised when he looked up from drinking his coffee to catch Tiffany sliding into the seat across from him. He hadn't taken acting classes or anything, but he thought he did pretty good with looking sad and slightly distraught that particular morning.

"I heard about you and Lisa, Jason." Tiffany reached across the table and covered his hand with her own. "I'm so sorry about what I'm sure you're going through." She looked him in the eye. "Her working as a porn star was too much for you to handle, huh?"

Playing his role, Jason frowned. "I don't want to talk about her or any of that, Tiffany."

"I imagine not." She gave his hand a squeeze. "You poor man you."

Jason sat there talking to Tiffany for almost a whole hour. By the time she stood up to leave, she had convinced him to go out with her to dinner that evening to get his mind off of things. According to Tiffany, keeping yourself occupied was the key to getting over a breakup.

Jason smiled to himself as he watched her walk away. *I think that was a success.*

Everybody who knew Jason and Lisa knew that Fridays were their date night. So, Carmen was surprised when Lisa called asking if she wanted to catch a movie. Carmen didn't mind going out with her girl — no, not in the slightest — because she didn't have anything better to do that evening herself. Although, she was surprised that Lisa wasn't preoccupied with Jason like usual.

Carmen hopped into Lisa's Jeep and they took off. Then, Carmen look across at the driver-side at her bestie and smiled. "Jason outta town or something, boo? That why y'all not going out tonight?"

"No, he's in town. But we broke up."

"What?!"

Lisa couldn't help but smile.

"Lord have mercy... You kidding... right?"

Lisa hit the interstate. "Nope."

"You and Jason broke up and you're not tore up about it... Are you in the middle of a mental breakdown, boo? Is that what I'm witnessing?"

Lisa laughed. "Naw. Lemme tell you a little story, but first I gotta get you to promise that not a word I'm about to tell you leaves this vehicle. Okay?"

After Lisa had finished filling Carmen in on their plan to trick Tiffany into a confession while Jason was wearing a wire tap while taping the whole thing, Carmen frowned. "It sure does sound like Tiffany is guilty as sin, but is Jason dating her a good idea?" She sucked her teeth. "I'd be worried if my man was wining and dining and running around with some other sista like they a couple."

Lisa didn't bat a lash. She said with confidence, "I trust my man, boo...and I prayed on it. It's gonna be alright."

Carmen looked at her girl out the side of her eye. She could tell from the look on Lisa's face that she felt like God would handle the situation. Lisa's strong, unwavering faith was admirable to Carmen — even in the crazy, messed up situation she was in.

Carmen finally sighed, "Alright, Lisa. I guess I better start praying on it, too."

Lisa finally grinned again. "Thank you, girl."

A whole two and a half weeks had flown by and Jason was now spending most of his free time with Tiffany. He and Lisa would talk for a little while every night before they both went to bed, but that was about the extent of their interactions. Tiffany never would've believed that they weren't still together otherwise. It was on week three that Lisa began getting the tiniest bit concerned about Jason and Tiffany's relationship.

Lisa, Carmen, and Carmen's housemate, Janelle, were sitting in a restaurant having dinner when Jason and Tiffany came in laughing and joking together. What really dug at Lisa is how Jason opened the door for Tiffany and escorted her inside — just like he'd always done for her.

When Janelle — who didn't know anything about the plan — leaned over the table and whispered, "Look at that trick with your ex, Lisa. Looks like he over you already", Lisa was through. To anybody looking in, it looked like Jason was in love with Tiffany or falling for her.

It also didn't help that Tiffany noticed Lisa sitting in the restaurant and pushed herself up on her tiptoes and gave Jason a kiss on his cheek. Then she glanced over and flashed Lisa a nasty look that clearly communicated: *Your man's mine now, trick.*

*Oh h to the naw*, Lisa thought to herself. It took Carmen placing her hand on Lisa's arm and shaking her head '*no*' to stop her from going over there.

"It ain't even worth it, boo," Carmen warned her girl. It's all in God's hands...right? Remember, you're trusting him for deliverance on all of this."

Janelle snickered. "It looks like the only thing being delivered is love bites between your ex and Tiffany, Lisa. I know you saved and all now, but I ain't. Want me to go over there and snatch that wig off her head, then push her in the face? She ain't even have to look at you all nice-nasty like she just did. That ish was uncalled for."

Carmen gave Janelle a look of warning. "We on parole, boo. Remember that, a'ight. You gonna be back in lock-up for mess like that."

Unfortunately for Janelle, she knew that her girl was right.

*Two Hours Later*:

Lisa pulled her Jeep into the driveway at the halfway house that Carmen and Janelle were living in. Janelle went ahead and went inside, while Carmen stayed in the Jeep — she wanted to shoot the breeze with Lisa for a few minutes.

Carmen looked over at her girl. "I'mma let you know right now that I didn't believe in this little idea that y'all had hatched up at first, boo. But God put it on my heart that y'all are about to have a breakthrough — that is if you don't drop the ball during the last inning." She looked at Lisa in warning. "Know what I mean?"

Lisa knew what she meant all right, but she couldn't clear the images of Jason and Tiffany looking like a real couple out her head. "All right, Carmen," she finally said.

Carmen opened the car door and got out. Before she walked away, she told her girl, "I'll be praying for you, boo."

"Thanks. I think I'm gonna need all the prayers I can get."

*Later on that Night*:

Lisa had been waiting all evening for Jason's call. She'd told herself that she was gonna play it cool once they got on the phone together, but unfortunately for her, he never did dial her number that evening. She knew she had the option of calling him to see what was up, but she was stubborn. "Imma see if he calls me," she whispered as she laid alone in her bed fuming. "That's what I'mma do."

By 1AM, she'd figured out that he wasn't gonna call her that night — which was a first since the day they'd gotten engaged. She was too upset over everything to ring his phone. She didn't even send him a text.

She closed her eyes and began talking to God about it all. Then she finally went to sleep.

# CHAPTER 14

When Lisa woke up the following morning, she had a renewed spirit about everything. She'd had a beautiful dream — one that she considered to be a vision. In her dream, she and Jason were lying in bed together on their wedding night. In Lisa's mind, that was God's way of telling her that everything would end up okay.

When Lisa had gone to bed the previous night, she'd had it on her brain to wake up that morning and take herself down to Jason's job and act the fool. She was newly saved — only a babe in Christ — so that type of behavior still wasn't quite above her yet.

Flipping pancakes on the stove, Diane looked over at her daughter and smiled. "You looking mighty chipper this morning, Lisa. God must be healing your broken heart. You must be getting over Jason."

Lisa had limited the number of people who she'd told about their plan. Her mama was a little bit on the gossipy side, so she'd known not to trust her with such sensitive information.

Lisa smiled. "God is good, mama. He supplies all our wants and needs. He really does. All we have to do is trust in him and never give up faith… And I mean *never*."

"That's sho nuff the truth, baby girl. And it sho is a good thing that the insurance company cut you that check to take care of everything that you lost in that fire."

Lisa nodded her head in agreement. "Yeah. I think the bakery is gonna end up better than it was before. I'm gonna be able to put my personal touch on everything. The Real Sweet Spot is gonna be blinging...from the floor to ceiling… But in a good kind of way. A stylish type of way. Nothing ghetto fabulous."

Diane chuckled. She knew her daughter. "I know it is, Lisa."

Lisa was still in the kitchen talking to her mama when someone began ringing the doorbell.

"I'll go get it, mama."

"Okay, honey."

As soon as Lisa pulled open the front door, Jason picked her up into his arms and began swinging her around. "It's all over, sweetheart! I got a confession last night! Tiffany told me everything. My partner is downtown finalizing the paperwork to pick her up for questioning today."

Lisa was overjoyed to hear that — and she was also thankful. She was happy that God had touched her heart and told her in her dream the previous night that everything was going to be okay. She knew there was a chance that she could've possibly lost everything if she'd acted out like she had intended on doing. *It wasn't gonna be pretty once I got downtown to the police station and started acting a fool. And it definitely wasn't gonna be pretty when I finally got my hands on Tiffany...not pretty at all.*

Grinning real hard, Jason continued speaking. "That's why I didn't call you last night — and I'm sorry for that. Tiffany invited me to stay over at her house. Once I got inside, she poured us drinks — I didn't have any in case you're wondering. She really began loosening up by her second glass of wine." He nodded his head and continued speaking. "It was an inside job, just like we'd suspected. She paid Big Ron's cousin, Tyrone, five-hundred dollars to burn your place down for her. Don't worry, we'll be picking him up, too."

He shook his head. "That girl's a real piece of work. She hated you with a passion, Bae, and she was willing to do some of anything to hurt you and bring you down."

Lisa grimaced. "Yeah. But God had my back. She must not realize how tight me and God are now."

Jason proceeded to pull his baby into a hug. He rested his chin on top of her curly head in contentment and smiled. "Yeah. No weapon formed against the righteous shall prosper, Bae. I love you, Lisa, with all my heart. I've missed you these past few weeks and I can barely wait till we're married."

"I love you, too, Jason. Now and for the rest of my life."

# 𝓔PILOGUE

A whole year had passed since the fire at The Real Sweet Spot. Just like Lisa had told her mother in her kitchen all those days ago, her bakery rose from the ashes more beautiful than anything she'd originally planned. It turned out that Janelle had been studying commercial interior design all the years she'd been in lockup. She'd collaborated with Lisa to make her bakery into something really special.

The Real Sweet Spot had even become a popular place for quite a few celebrities. A famous internationally known wrapper had happened to drop into her place one day six months ago. He'd ended up telling all his friends about it. Things really took off from there. Business was really booming — so much so that Jason had quit his job as a police detective. He and Lisa were now running the bakery full-time together.

As for Tiffany, she'd had her day in court. She'd been convicted of first-degree arson — which had come with a fifty-thousand dollar fine — and a few other charges. She'd received a nine year sentence. She was now spending her days at the Georgia prison that Carmen and Janelle had gotten out of.

As for Carmen, she'd found a man of her own and was happily married. God had recently granted Lisa with the gift of prophecy. She'd seen in a vision that Janelle was going to get married soon, too — and to a man. Seeing that she considered herself to be a lesbian for life, Janelle had laughed at that. It hadn't fazed Lisa though. She knew what God had shown her.

Lisa smiled as a good looking brotha approached the front counter and handed Janelle a cupcake to ring up for him. The way that he was checking her friend out wasn't lost on Lisa, and the way that Janelle was being all bashful around him wasn't lost on her either. She smiled. I think your lesbian days are about to be over Janelle.

Jason approached from behind and placed his arms around his wife's waist. Her belly was just beginning to show from the fruits of their lovemaking.

He leaned into her ear and whispered, "You wanna play hooky and go home for a little while, Mrs. Mathis?"

She knew exactly what he had in mind once they got home, and she was all for it. Lisa loved the way Jason loved her. He kept her well satisfied in the bedroom, and she was sure she did the same for him. Nothing was off limits between the two… After all, they were married.

She giggled like a schoolgirl. Then she said in a

husky whisper, "Give me two and a half minutes. I'll be outside waiting for you by the Benz."

As Jason collected his things to leave the bakery for the day, he had a satisfied smile on his face. *Thank you Lord for sending me my soulmate. For years, I was praying to meet her. She must have stumbled into my prayer. I'm going to love and cherish her forever.*

## FIRSTMAN PUBLICATIONS

Thank you for reading this book. On the following pages, we've provided previews of other great books by this author — stories that we feel you will thoroughly enjoy. Also, feel free to visit our website at WWW.FIRSTMANBOOKS.COM to:

*Register for FREE offers

*Sign up for our mailing list

*Check out additional great books by other Firstman Publications featured authors

*Order a FREE catalog

### OTHER BOOKS BY WAYNE COLLEY

Trouble All In My Way

God Ain't Playing

A Diva's Prayer

# STUMBLING INTO A PRAYER

## Other Wayne Colley Books You May Enjoy

**Firstman Publications**     www.firstmanbooks.com

# STUMBLING INTO A PRAYER

DATE: _____

**Firstman Publications, P.O. Box 14302, Greensboro NC 27415**

TOLL FREE: 1-800-729-4849    www.firstmanbooks.com    Email: fmp@firstmanbooks.com

**BILL TO**

NAME _____ COMPANY _____
ADDRESS _____
CITY _____ ST _____ ZIP _____
Phone( ____ ) _____ Fax( ____ ) _____ E-Mail _____

**SHIP TO**

NAME _____ COMPANY _____
ADDRESS _____
CITY _____ ST _____ ZIP _____
Phone( ____ ) _____ Fax( ____ ) _____ E-Mail _____

| Book Title | Item Code | How Many | Price Each | Total Price |
|---|---|---|---|---|
|  |  |  |  |  |
|  |  |  |  |  |
|  |  |  |  |  |
|  |  |  |  |  |
|  |  |  |  |  |
|  |  |  |  |  |

**TOTAL AMOUNT**

**SHIPPING:** $3 for one book. $1 each additional book.

**SALES TAX:** N.C. Add 7%

**GRAND TOTAL**

☐ Money Order enclosed payable to Firstman Publications  -OR-

Credit Card Number _____
Name on Card _____
Expiration Date _____ CVV Code _____
Signature _____

You may photocopy this page and use the copies as your fax or mail order forms.

# STUMBLING INTO A PRAYER

# STUMBLING INTO A PRAYER

Made in the USA
Lexington, KY
20 October 2018